Sweet Fire and Stone

A SWEET COVE, MASSACHUSETTS

COZY MYSTERY

BOOK 7

J.A. WHITING

To hear about new books and book sales, please sign up for my mailing list at: www.jawhitingbooks.com

For my family, with love

CHAPTER 1

Josh Williams sat on a stool and leaned forward with his elbow on the counter. His hand wrapped around the steaming white mug of coffee as he dreamily watched Angie Roseland bustling around the new bake shop. The usual morning chatter from the early customers filled the space. An occasional burst of laughter punctuated the conversations and discussions that bounced in the air.

The old pewter chandelier from Angie's previous shop had been salvaged and now hung from the new café's ceiling and its pieces of cut glass and crystal sparkled and glimmered over the people gathered at tables and the customers standing in line at the counter. The shop, located in part of the Victorian mansion that Angie had inherited and now shared with her three sisters, had been open for two months and business was booming.

Angie had her honey-blonde hair pulled into a high bun and a tiny loose strand framed the side of her face. As she reached for a blueberry muffin in

1

the glass case, she caught Josh staring at her and she stood straight and cocked her head. "What?"

Josh shook his head slowly, his blue eyes twinkling at his girlfriend. "Just enjoying the view."

Angie's cheeks flushed and a little smile played over her lips. A tingle of warmth spread through her body.

"Leave Angie alone." Courtney winked. Angie's youngest sister placed a warm carrot muffin onto the small white plate that sat on the counter in front of Josh. "You're interfering with her ability to work."

"I'll tell Rufus the same thing about you when I see him lurking around in your candy store," Josh joked.

Courtney's face lost its smile and a gloomy expression darkened her eyes. Walking into the kitchen, she pulled the pale blue apron over her head. She'd worked for two hours at the bake shop to help with the early rush and had to get to her candy store in the center of town to open for the day.

Josh looked blankly at the youngest Roseland sister and then turned to Angie for help. "What did I say?"

Angie stepped closer and whispered. "Rufus is going back to England soon and Courtney isn't very happy about it."

Courtney's boyfriend, Rufus Fudge, had been interning at Sweet Cove attorney Jack Ford's office for several months and in a week he would be returning to England for his final term of studies.

"Oh, right." Josh glanced towards the kitchen with a sympathetic look. "I forgot Rufus was leaving this month."

Angie carried a takeout cup of coffee over to one of the customers. "Here you are, Professor Tyler." Professor Michael Tyler was tall and slender with a full head of white hair. He had been into the bake shop several mornings in a row and had chatted with Angie on each visit. He was a retired history professor from New York City and was visiting the seacoast towns on the North Shore of Massachusetts. The man had written extensively on the Salem Witch hysteria of the 1600s and was conducting research on how nearby towns were influenced and affected.

"Thank you, Angie." The professor had the same thing each morning, a black coffee and a chocolate croissant and he took a coffee away with him when he left. "Your croissants are the best I've ever had and I've traveled extensively all over the world." He lifted his cup to her in a salute.

Angie chuckled. "That's very high praise. Thank you."

"Tell me. Might there be a room available here at the inn? The resort is fine, but I do enjoy staying at bed and breakfasts and historic homes."

"I'm not sure. It's been busy. My sister, Ellie, is still serving breakfast in the B and B dining room if you'd like to go by when you're finished and ask her." Angie smiled. "Tell her I sent you in."

The man paid and left the bakery promising to be back the next day. As Angie was clearing the table, an elderly couple entered the shop and Louisa, Angie's employee, greeted them and helped them to a table by the windows. The gray-haired man wore a heavy wool black coat that hung on him as if it were several sizes too big. The woman had pasty skin and slits for eyes. Her shoulders drooped forward as if they'd had enough of years maintaining straight posture and had given up. The man said something to Louisa and she shut the window for them.

The early October light filtered softly through the glass. Louisa had worked at a café in Coveside for a few years and needed a change. Angie was happy to have such an experienced worker join her at her new bake shop.

Angie walked to the cash register to ring up another customer. As the older couple settled in their chairs, she made eye contact with them and gave a welcoming smile. They turned away so deliberately that Angie was taken aback.

"Angie?" Betty Hayes, a Sweet Cove Realtor, stood in front of the counter.

Angie shook herself. "What can I get you?"

Betty gave her order and chattered nonstop with Josh while she waited for her takeout mocha latte. The busy Realtor usually sat and talked with the

bake shop regulars, but today she had an early appointment and couldn't linger. Angie was still wondering about the older couple's behavior. She snapped the lid on the extra-large mocha and carried it to Betty.

"Don't turn around," Angie said, "but do you know the couple who came in right before you did and sat down by the window?"

Betty almost turned her head, but she stopped herself. She handed Angie a ten dollar bill and leaned forward. "The grouchy ones?" Betty didn't wait for a response. "I know them. I recently rented them a house over on Greenhill Road. They were not easy to work with, but they paid cash for six months rent up front, so I put up with them."

Angie handed her some change. "They're new to town then?"

"They are." Betty sniffed. "And not a welcome addition."

Josh swiveled on his stool with his coffee in his hand and nonchalantly looked over the crowd of people sitting at tables. When he spotted the couple by the windows being served by Louisa, he swiveled back. "Those two have been staying at the resort. They're always complaining, never satisfied. I can't say we'll be sorry to see them go."

"Exactly." Betty picked up the takeout cup.

"Where did they move from?" Angie started down the counter to wait on other customers.

"They must have told me." Betty's forehead

scrunched up in thought. "I can't recall. See you later tonight. I'm bringing a mashed potato casserole." Betty whirled and headed for the exit. She was dating Victor Finch, a family friend of the Roseland sisters, and tonight was "family" dinner night at the sisters' Victorian mansion.

Betty's answer about not being able to recall where the elderly couple had moved from caused a skitter of nervousness to flit over Angie's skin. She couldn't understand why two grumpy new customers were bothering her so much. When she finished filling multiple takeout orders, she slid back to stand at the counter in front of Josh. He noticed her faraway look. "What's wrong?"

Angie let out a little sigh and kept her voice low. "I know it's silly, but for some reason, that couple makes me really uneasy."

Josh smiled. "They're just sullen and unhappy. Some people are miserable. Try not to let their nasty moods bother you." He reached his hand across the granite surface and Angie squeezed his fingers. She made eye contact with her boyfriend and warmth flooded through her body. Josh always made her feel better.

"Are you coming to dinner night?" Angie still held the handsome man's hand.

"I wouldn't miss it." Josh smiled. "I'd better get back to the resort. Davis will be tapping his toe waiting for me." Josh and his older brother, Davis, owned the Sweet Cove Resort, among other properties, and were also real estate developers. The two brothers did not share the same outlook on life. Davis Williams was all-business and Angie couldn't remember ever seeing a smile on his face. Josh believed in hard work and setting and achieving goals, but he also understood the importance of enjoying life with someone he loved. Josh kissed Angie's fingers and headed out the door of the bake shop just as Ellie Roseland came out of the kitchen and strode over to the pastry case.

"That new guest is driving me crazy." She peered into the case, her long blonde hair falling over her shoulder, and removed a slice of chocolate mousse cake from the shelf. Ellie ran the Victorian's bed and breakfast inn. "He is so demanding. I wish I didn't rent the room to him for so many weeks. Imagine ... chocolate mousse cake for breakfast." She shook her head and straightened up, and then she froze in position for a moment staring off into space.

Angie gave Ellie the eye just as her fraternal twin sister, Jenna, hurried by carrying a tray of dirty dishes. The diamond of her pretty engagement ring sparkled under the light of the bake shop's chandelier. Jenna paused on her way to the kitchen, cocked her head, and stared at Ellie. "What's wrong with you?"

Ellie blinked. "I don't know. I felt something funny." She reached for a small tray, placed the plate with the slice of mousse cake on it, and hurried back towards the main kitchen. "It was nothing. By the way, Mr. Finch said the cats have been causing a ruckus trying to sneak into the kitchen and get out here all morning."

Jenna and Angie shared a worried look. Along with the mansion, Angie had inherited a huge orange Maine Coon cat and a few months ago, a stray black cat showed up on their doorstep and the sisters took her in. Since they'd all been together, the two felines had a hand, or paw, in helping the Roselands solve several mysteries. Angie's throat tightened as she wondered why on earth the two cats were so determined to come into the bake shop.

A customer approached the counter and when Angie turned to take the order, she caught the older couple sitting by the window scowling in her direction. They quickly averted their gazes, but the expression on their faces sent a shudder down Angie's back as if an icy cold, bony finger was tracing along her spine.

Ever since the summer, things had been quiet in the seaside town of Sweet Cove, Massachusetts. Angie got the feeling that was about to change.

CHAPTER 2

Angie came down the carved wooden staircase to the foyer of the Victorian. A round polished wooden table stood on a burgundy, green, and cream colored rug and a cut-glass vase of orange and yellow Gerber daisies had been placed in its center.

Courtney was in the dining room setting the table and without looking up, she said, "What's cookin,' Sis?"

"Not much." Angie yawned and stretched. "How was the candy store?" Courtney and Mr. Finch owned a candy store together in the center of town.

"Busy. Even though it's October, things are going strong."

"People are traveling to see the fall foliage and they stop here along the way. The B and B isn't showing any signs of slowing down either." Angie went to the buffet and opened a drawer to remove the silverware. She started around the table placing forks, knives, and spoons beside each of the plates.

A ceramic pumpkin filled with colorful fall flowers sat in the center of the dining table.

Mr. Finch, leaning on his cane, entered from the hallway and greeted the sisters. Euclid, the orange cat, and Circe, the black cat, trailed behind him. Finch carried a platter of cookies in his hand which he set down on the side table. The older man was dressed in a pale orange shirt and tweed jacket. He wore a black bow tie with tiny orange pumpkins printed on the fabric.

"You're looking dapper, Mr. Finch." Angie smiled at him.

"A bow tie?" Courtney eyed the man's choice of neckwear.

"It is in honor of Jack's birthday." Finch straightened his shoulders. "I have the very same bow tie wrapped in a gift bag for the young attorney." Ellie's boyfriend, Jack Ford, was known for always wearing a bow tie.

The sisters had started a new tradition of having their boyfriends, Mr. Finch, and Betty to dinner once a month and since Jack's birthday was coming up, they decided to celebrate the occasion at tonight's get-together.

"But Jack told us no birthday gifts." Courtney placed wine glasses at each setting.

"I am an old man, Miss Courtney." Finch's eyes twinkled. "I now have the liberty to do what I think appropriate."

The cats jumped up on the China cabinet and

settled down to watch the evening's festivities. Angie eyed the animals. "Ellie said the cats were trying to get into the bake shop this morning?"

Mr. Finch sat down in one of the dining chairs. "They were most adamant about it. When I came in for breakfast this morning, they were both standing at attention at the doors to the commercial kitchen howling. I peeked in there to see if an emergency was taking place." Finch lived in the house behind the Roseland's Victorian and he often had his meals with them or came over to have coffee in the kitchen and read his newspaper. When the mansion was being renovated to house the bake shop, the large kitchen space had been designed so that the commercial side could be closed off with pocket doors to keep it separate from the family side of the space.

"Did the cats settle down once you came in?" Angie asked.

"It took some time for them to stop carrying on. I wondered what they were going on about." Finch made eye contact with Angie. "I found it unnerving."

Angie sat down next to Finch and told him about the elderly couple who visited the bake shop early in the day and how they made her nervous. "Betty said that they've recently moved to town."

Finch had his hands closed over the top of his cane. He glanced up at the cats.

Courtney placed some candles next to the

ceramic pumpkin centerpiece. "Sometimes people just have an aversion to somebody. It's a personality conflict or whatever."

Finch and Angie didn't say anything which caused Courtney to look up. Seeing their expressions made her eyebrows shoot up. "Oh. You think something's up?"

The cats hissed.

Ellie carried a birthday cake into the dining room and stopped short. She took a quick look up at the cats, faced Courtney, and frowned. "What do you mean something's up?"

Angie reminded Ellie how she'd had a funny feeling when she came into the bake shop. She told her sister about the older couple and how their presence had bothered her.

"My feeling didn't mean anything." Ellie tried to brush it off. "I get feelings all the time."

"Really? *All* the time?" Courtney narrowed her eyes.

"Well, sometimes." Ellie put the cake on the buffet table.

"What did you feel?" Angie looked nervous. She clasped her hands in her lap to keep them from fidgeting. Since moving to Sweet Cove in the spring, the four Roseland sisters discovered that they each possessed some paranormal powers which they were trying to adjust to and incorporate into their lives ... some of them with more success than others.

Ellie turned and swallowed. Her brow scrunched up in thought. "I don't know." She crossed her arms over her chest in a defensive posture. "Like ... something dangerous was in the air." She gave a shrug. "But that was silly, it didn't mean anything. You shouldn't pay any attention to it." She lowered her voice. "I'd been complaining about the new guest who's staying with us. He's a pain. He follows me around and asks me a million questions, but when I ask *him* anything he replies with something vague. He makes me uncomfortable. Maybe that was causing me some anxiety and I confused it with a sense of danger." She dismissively batted the air with her hand. "Not everything is a warning of impending doom."

Angie and Finch exchanged skeptical looks.

As she turned to head back to the kitchen, Ellie said, "Your Professor Tyler stopped in. Another guest checked out unexpectedly so I was able to give him a room."

Finch asked about Professor Tyler and Angie filled him in on the new guest and his research into the Salem Witch Trials. She glanced at the hallway to be sure Ellie wasn't in earshot. "I think Ellie needs to pay more attention to her feelings."

Finch nodded.

Courtney moved around the table so she could take the water glasses out of the China cabinet. "The cats seem to be agitated so I'm inclined to ignore Ellie and lean towards thinking that something is up."

Finch gave a little tap on the rug with his cane. "Time will tell."

"We should be careful though." Courtney carried two crystal goblets to the table. "We need to be on guard just in case."

Anxiety swirled through Angie's body. Lately, everything had been going so smoothly. There had been no murders or deaths in Sweet Cove since the summer so it hadn't been necessary for the police to call in the sisters and their abilities to consult for any cases. The bake shop was doing well. The October days had been warm and pleasant. Angie wished things could stay as they were, but she knew deep down that something was brewing. "I want to find out more about that older couple who visited the shop this morning."

Finch agreed. "Miss Betty will probably be able to tell you a bit about them since I believe she worked closely with the couple to find a house. She complained about their unpleasant personalities to me. It must be the same couple who visited your bake shop this morning."

As if on cue, the doorbell rang and Betty opened the front door and rushed into the foyer carrying a casserole dish. "I was afraid I was late." She pushed the dish into Angie's hands and nearly crushed Mr. Finch in a bear hug. She kissed the top of the man's head. "You look so handsome in a bow tie, Victor." She batted her eyes at him. "Maybe you should wear one more often." Finch blushed when Betty gave a girlish giggle.

Courtney stared at the woman and shook her head. Finch, a gentle and kind man, was slight and unsteady due to an injury of long ago while Betty, who carried some extra pounds, was like a force-five hurricane hitting the room. The sisters were still amazed that Betty and Finch were a couple, but the two were practically giddy in each other's company and the girls loved that the older man and the successful Realtor were in love.

"I need a sip of wine." Betty hurried to the sideboard and poured some merlot into a glass. She looked sweetly at Finch. "Would you like a glass, Victor?"

"I'll wait until dinner, thank you." Finch beamed at the woman.

Angie stood to help Courtney finish setting the table. She addressed Betty. "What do you know about the couple you rented the Greenhill Road house to?"

Betty scowled. "They were royal pains. They complained about everything. I never thought I'd find them a house they wanted." She took a gulp from her glass and topped it off.

Courtney eyed Betty. The woman seemed distressed discussing the older couple. "Were they just the usual pains or was there something else about them that bothered you?"

Betty stared at the youngest Roseland sister.

"What do you mean?"

"You seem nervous talking about them."

Euclid stood up on the China cabinet and listened intently to the discussion.

Betty's cheeks went red. "I'm not nervous." She blinked. "Why would I be?"

"What specifically did they complain about?" Angie asked calmly.

Betty bustled over to Mr. Finch and sat next to him. "The house was ugly ... the garden was wrong ... the house was too close to town ... the house was too far from town. I couldn't get a handle on what they wanted."

"Where did they come from?" Angie's eyes were like lasers.

Betty pondered. "Hmm. I don't recall."

"What are their names?"

Betty opened her mouth to speak. She screwed up her face. "Um...." Betty gave a nervous laugh. "My." She looked at Finch. "Did I mention their names to you?"

Finch shook his head.

"Well, how funny. It's slipped my mind." Betty put her hand to the side of her face. "Oh well, it will come to me." She tried to brush off her forgetfulness.

Courtney sidled up next to Angie and raised an eyebrow. "This is odd. Betty recently worked with that couple. How could she just forget their names?"

"I have no idea." Angie's heart sank.

CHAPTER 3

The doorbell rang, and on her way to answer it, Courtney smiled. "Maybe all of this means we're going to have a new mystery to solve. We haven't had one for weeks." She beamed with excitement. Courtney was the sister who loved being involved in mysteries and using her newly-discovered and developing paranormal powers which the sisters had inherited from their grandmother. "Down on the beach." Jacob pointed ahead to the path at the edge of Anna's property that led down the rocky coast to a slip of sandy beach.

Angie hoped her youngest sister was wrong, but a mystery might be just the thing to keep Courtney from focusing so closely on Rufus's departure back to England.

One by one, the men arrived and the group sat down to their dinner of pot roast, spinach and cheese empanadas, roasted green beans, a rice and nut medley, and Betty's potato casserole.

Jack Ford admired Mr. Finch's bow tie which immediately started a round of teasing for his

choice to always wear the more formal-looking neckwear.

"I prefer the look," Jack sniffed. "I think it finishes an outfit and gives me a professional appearance."

Rufus passed the platter of green beans to Jack. "Don't you mean it gives you the appearance of an old nerd?"

Narrowing his eyes at the young legal intern, Jack accepted the platter. "Remind me. When are you finally leaving my office and returning to Oxford?"

The others chuckled at the friendly banter between the two men, but a shadow passed over Courtney's face at the mention of Rufus's leaving.

Conversation turned to the beautiful October weather, the upcoming Sweet Cove fall festival, and how business was still strong in town despite the end of summer.

"Miss Angie's bake shop is booming," Mr. Finch said. "The candy store is as busy as ever and the bed and breakfast rooms are all full."

Jenna smiled. "Tom's busy with construction projects and the coming holiday season is always my best time of year for jewelry orders and sales."

"We should all be busy until Christmas." Ellie reached over and straightened Jack's tie. He took her hand for a moment and held it tight which caused his cheeks to blush. Ellie continued, "Then we should take a vacation. We all need it."

A man's voice called from the stairs. "Miss Roseland."

Ellie cringed and rolled her eyes at the sound, but turned towards the staircase with a pleasant smile on her face. "I thought you'd gone out, Mr. Withers."

"I changed my plans. I've been out all afternoon so I decided to stay in this evening." Mr. Withers, the B and B guest who had been driving Ellie crazy, seemed to be in his early seventies. He had a sharp, bird-like nose, dark blue eyes, and a skinny face. His limbs were gangly and thin and he had long bony fingers. Ellie described him to her sisters as a mutant elf, but who was lacking in the pleasant personality one might expect in such a creature. The man strode to the dining table with a spring in his step and greeted the people sitting around it. Introductions went around the table.

Ellie took a breath. "Would you care to join us for dinner?" She hoped he would answer in the negative.

"I would love to." Withers glanced about for a place to sit.

Courtney stood and went to the China cabinet for another place setting while Tom picked up a chair and carried it to the table for the man. Ellie nodded to the far end where Mr. Finch was sitting. Tom placed the extra chair and Mr. Withers joined the group.

"Always room for one more," Mr. Finch declared

with a smile.

Withers's bushy gray brows seemed to dance over his eyes. "It's most appreciated." He reached for the platter of sliced pot roast and addressed Mr. Finch. "How long are you staying here at the inn?"

Mr. Finch explained that he was a permanent fixture at the Victorian despite living in his own home directly behind the B and B.

Withers bent over his dinner plate. "How can I make such an arrangement for myself?"

Ellie's face paled thinking about having Withers around for more than a few weeks.

Jenna nodded towards Mr. Finch with a smile. "I'm afraid this man is a once-in-a-lifetime exception."

"Pity." Withers sipped the wine that Courtney had placed in front of him. "Delicious meal. My compliments to the chef."

"Where are you from, Mr. Withers?" Jenna asked.

"All over." He didn't look up, just kept working on his dinner. "I don't stay anywhere for very long."

"Why not?" Courtney stared at the man.

Withers straightened and looked across the table at Courtney. He had piercing dark blue-gray eyes. "It is the nature of my work."

"Are you in sales?" Betty's eyes brightened. She loved chattering with other people who worked in sales.

Withers gave Betty a little smile as he picked up his knife and began to cut his pot roast. "Something similar."

Betty frowned at the cryptic remark. She was about to ask another question when Withers said, "I hear that real estate is doing quite well again."

That was all Betty needed to start on a long explanation of the state of home sales both nationally and in the state of Massachusetts.

Angie eyed Withers. She knew that the man had cleverly and deliberately turned the conversation away from inquiries about himself to a topic that would get Betty talking. Angie glanced across the table to her twin sister and Jenna gave the slightest of nods indicating that she too had picked up on Withers' deflection.

When Betty paused for a breath, Jenna turned the attention back on Withers. "Did you grow up in New England, Mr. Withers?" she smiled sweetly.

"I wasn't that lucky."

Jenna realized that her question should have been more open-ended in order to get a more detailed answer.

"Do you have family?" Courtney watched the man's face. She did not care for the man's evasive replies and was starting not to trust him.

"Again, I was not so lucky." Withers looked at Jenna and Tom. "I hear the two of you are engaged. Congratulations."

Jenna blinked in surprise.

Tom smiled and thanked the man for his well wishes. "We've recently purchased a house. It needs a lot of work."

Before Tom could continue, Withers spoke. "Miss Roseland told me that you bought a house a couple of doors down from here, the old Stenmark place."

"*What* place?" Tom looked puzzled.

Withers raised his eyes from his plate. His lips were pinched tightly together. He swallowed. "Stenmark. The Stenmark place."

Tom and Jenna glanced over to Betty since she was the one who sold the house to them.

Betty's cheeks flushed and she stammered. "There wasn't any information about the house. Only the past owner's name and it wasn't Stenmark. The place had been abandoned for years. The town owned it. I don't know any history."

"How do you know that someone named Stenmark was a previous owner?" Jenna asked Withers.

All eyes turned to the man.

Withers cleared his throat. "I love old houses. It's an avocation of mine. I enjoy reading about early America, especially the towns of New England, the old families, their homes."

"You've read about our house?" Tom questioned.

"Yes." Withers nodded. "Just a few words." He pointed to the mashed potato casserole. "May I have a bit more?"

23

Tom was eager to know more about their recently acquired home. "What can you tell us about our house?" He passed Withers the casserole dish.

"Nothing. I only read the name of the original owner and that the house was one of the first homes built on this street. Perhaps you'd be so kind to show it to me one day?"

"We'd be glad to." Tom gave a nod. "How long will you be here at the B and B?"

"Until the end of October." Withers took a long sip of his wine.

"You've planned a long visit in town," Tom observed.

"I'm using the Victorian as a home-base to visit the seacoast towns from Boston to Maine."

"It's a very pleasant time of year to do that," Finch said.

Withers looked at Finch. "Are you still working, Mr. Finch, or have you retired?"

Finch placed his fork on his plate. "Miss Courtney and I own the candy shop in the center of town."

"So you've lived here for some time, I assume."

"Not quite a year."

"Where do you hail from then?" Withers lifted his napkin to his lips.

"Chicago."

Angie noticed that Finch was only answering with direct replies and was not elaborating.

Withers finished off his glass of wine. "You had a candy store in Chicago?"

The two men made eye contact.

Finch could feel Euclid staring down at them from his perch on top of the China cabinet. "I was a fortune-teller when I lived in Chicago."

Withers gave Finch a wide-eyed look, then supposing the man was joshing with him, he threw his head back and laughed. He clapped Finch on the shoulder. "You had me for a minute." Withers shook his head as the other male guests around the table chuckled at Finch's remark. The sisters remained quiet knowing that Finch really *had* worked as a fortune-teller.

Finch lifted the bottle of red wine and held it out to the man. "Would you care for more wine?"

"Indeed I would." The man reached for the bottle that was in Finch's hand.

Mr. Finch could occasionally discover something about a person if they both held an object simultaneously. For only a second, Withers and Finch held the bottle of Cabernet at the same time, but it was enough.

As Finch placed his hands in his lap, he glanced at Angie. The tiniest of smiles played over his lips.

CHAPTER 4

After finishing the meal, singing happy birthday wishes to Jack, and devouring the delicious cake Angie had baked, the guests returned to their homes. Mr. Withers climbed the stairs to his room, and the girls and Mr. Finch retired to the family room at the back of the house. Euclid sat next to Courtney in the easy chair, his orange plume of a tail occasionally flicking against her cheek. Although Circe was curled on top of Finch's lap, the black cat was alert and listening to the humans' conversation. Ellie came into the room carrying a bowl of roasted tomato soup. "You're back." She sat down next to Finch. "Did you figure out what was happening with the chief's aunt?"

Angie smiled at Finch. "How clever of you to tell Mr. Withers that you had been a fortune-teller when you lived in Chicago."

"I thought it best to throw the man off and lower his defenses by telling him something outlandish just before we held the bottle together." Finch actually had been a fortune-teller during the last years he'd lived in the windy city, but the sisters, Police Chief Martin, and Jenna's fiancé, Tom, were the only ones in Sweet Cove who knew of the man's skills.

"We only held the bottle together for a moment and I wasn't able to pick up on much, but I'm hoping that perhaps since he will be staying here for several weeks, I will have the opportunity to discover more." Finch gently ran his hand over the black cat's velvet fur and she purred.

Courtney's eyes were bright. "Tell us what you sensed from Withers."

"I could not determine if the man's reason for visiting the area was true or false. However, I picked up that he is clearly hiding something from us."

"Are we in danger?" Ellie twisted the ends of her long hair.

"Unknown." Finch's eyebrows pinched together in a scowl. "Nothing imminent was evident, but...."

"But what?" Jenna slid a couple of inches across the sofa cushion so that her shoulder touched Angie's.

Finch looked over the top of his glasses. "But the man has a mission and it involves all of us."

Euclid let out a long, low hiss.

Ellie's hand flew to her throat. "Oh, no. What does he want with us?"

Finch took his glasses off and wiped the lenses with a handkerchief. "That is yet to be determined,

Miss Ellie."

"Then we'd better be on guard." Angie's lips turned down.

"That must be why he follows me around, asking all kinds of questions." Ellie stood and started pacing up and down by the windows. "I thought he was just an annoying, inquisitive pest, but he must have ulterior motives for interrogating me."

"Does this guy have some connection to the older couple who were in the bake shop this morning?" Courtney adjusted her position in the chair to give Euclid more room.

"Good point," Jenna said. "Three people show up in Sweet Cove around the same time and make us feel uneasy. Maybe they know each other? Maybe they're up to something together?"

"We need to find out more about the couple." Angie's face clouded. "It was very strange that Betty couldn't even recall their names."

"In Miss Betty's defense," Finch offered, "she has been busier than ever and is juggling many different clients at the moment. It was probably a momentary lapse."

"*Or,* that older couple put a spell on her so she wouldn't remember any particulars about them." Courtney's voice was excited.

"Oh, God." Ellie looked like she might start to cry.

"Betty can always look up the information in her file." Jenna turned to Angie. "Do you think we should tell Chief Martin our concerns?"

Angie sighed. "I think we'd better. I'll talk to him tomorrow morning when he comes into the bake shop."

"Do you think this has something to do with Tom's and my new house?" Jenna's eyes were as wide as saucers. "Withers brought it up at dinner."

"I bet he knows more about your house than he's saying." Angie's face hardened. "I got the sense that the name 'Stenmark' slipped out by accident."

Courtney narrowed her eyes. "I got the same impression. Withers tried to cover his mistake by claiming that he didn't know much about the house, but I bet he knows plenty."

"You know what...?" Jenna looked pensive. "When I was working at the house this afternoon I had the oddest feeling that someone was watching me."

Ellie stopped pacing and stared at her sister. She asked in a whisper, "Was Tom there with you?"

Jenna shook her head. "I was alone. I was working on sanding the staircase and the front door was open. My back was to the door." The muscle in her cheek twitched. "I got the weirdest sensation that someone was standing on the porch watching me. Tom loves to sneak up on me sometimes so I thought it was him about to play a prank. I turned around fast to try and startle him, but no one was there."

"Did you check the porch?" Angie asked.

"Yeah. I went out and looked around." Jenna's blue eyes stared across the room. "I stood on the porch and glanced about the yard." She gave a shrug. "Then I thought maybe a squirrel or a chipmunk had just scurried across the porch and made me think someone was there." She tapped her forefinger on her chin. "Looking back on it, I guess someone could have hidden from me in the front bushes."

Finch cocked his head. "Was the sensation you had ghostly in any way, Miss Jenna?"

The pretty brunette thought for a moment. "I don't think so. It didn't feel the same as when I see a spirit."

Courtney sat up. "That happened this afternoon, right? Didn't Mr. Withers say he decided to stay in this evening because he'd been out all afternoon?"

Ellie's lips pressed together tightly and then she said, "That's exactly what he told me." Her cheeks flushed with anger as she turned to Jenna. "Was Withers watching you?" Even though Ellie always wanted to stay far away from investigating cases and criminals, she had an iron will when it came to protecting the people she loved.

Worry washed over Jenna's face. "Maybe I'll take the cats with me next time I go over to work on the house."

"You shouldn't be there alone right now." Ellie went back to the sofa and sat on the edge of the seat. "Maybe the cats aren't enough protection."

Euclid eyed Ellie and hissed.

Ellie gave the huge orange cat a look. "I'm just saying that maybe a human should go along with Jenna, too. Safety in numbers."

Euclid turned away with a scowl.

"I love my house." Worry lines furrowed Jenna's forehead. "I won't be intimidated by some nut who wants to stare at it ... or at me."

Angie gave her sister's hand a squeeze. "You need to be careful. The nut might have plans to do more than just stare."

Jenna blew out a sigh. "I'll be sure to keep the doors locked."

"You might want to get some pepper spray." Courtney pulled an elastic off her wrist and twisted her hair into a high, loose bun. "We need to get on this before things get ahead of us."

"I agree." Worry was pulsing through Angie's body making her feel anxious and agitated. Making a plan would give her a sense of control over what was going on. "There are three things we need to look into."

"First, we need to find out about Mr. Withers and what he's up to." Ellie's face was pinched. "I will be very careful in my conversations with him, and from now on, I'm going to be the one who asks him a bunch of questions."

Trying to lighten the mood, Angie nodded at Ellie and smiled. "Now we have a secret agent on the case." She turned to Jenna. "We also need to find out about the older couple who just rented the house in Sweet Cove. Can you get away from your jewelry shop later in the afternoon tomorrow? I'd like to talk to Betty about them and if we have time, we can go to the town hall and look up the real estate transactions on your house. See if a Stenmark once owned it."

"I'll start work on my jewelry orders early in the morning so I can get things done by the afternoon."

"And I'll watch the shop for you when you go out," Ellie said and then asked Angie, "You said there are three things we need to do. What's the third thing?"

"We need to find out why Withers seems so interested in Jenna and Tom's house."

Courtney rubbed her hands together, stood up, and headed towards the family room door for the kitchen. "Anyone want something to eat? I'm getting a snack. The excitement of a new case always makes me hungry."

Mr. Finch requested a large bowl of buttered popcorn which elicited stares from the four sisters. He gave a slight shrug of his shoulder. "I believe I am succumbing to stress eating."

Ellie's jaw dropped. "You never stress eat. Why are these things causing you more worry than usual?" She swallowed hard, afraid of the answer.

Mr. Finch gently scratched Circe's cheeks. "Every day there are currents that travel on the air. Bad things, good things, but they usually balance

out.   This morning when the cats were so desperately trying to get into the bake shop, the air was more turbulent, like the strong, early waves of a coming storm." .

"You've felt these waves before though, right?" Angie was seeking some reassurance. "We've been involved with lots of bad cases. You must have felt this sort of thing before."

Mr. Finch's eyes looked watery.   He didn't answer right away.

Circe stood up on the man's lap and put her front paws on his chest.

Finch shifted his eyes to the sweet creature. In a soft, quiet voice he said, "This coming storm holds danger, and this time ...it's aimed at us."

CHAPTER 5

Angie and Jenna walked into Betty's real estate agency. When the girls called the office earlier in the day, the receptionist told them that Betty would be back at 4pm, but as they glanced around the place there was no sign of the energetic broker so they took seats in the waiting area. The late afternoon October sunlight streamed in through the large glass windows and warmed the girls.

"I could fall asleep in this chair." Angie leaned back against the soft mocha fabric and closed her eyes for a few moments. "Getting the bake shop ready and finally opening it has me worn out."

"Well, you'd better get your energy back because I think you're going to need it." Jenna's eyes bugged out when she saw two people standing on the sidewalk by the windows. "Don't look now, but your two biggest fans are outside."

"You're kidding. Twice in one day?" Angie pushed herself to attention and started to swivel around.

"Don't turn your head. They're looking right in

here." Jenna kept the older couple in her peripheral vision so they wouldn't see her watching them. They had made their second appearance in two days at the bake shop that morning where they continued their not-so-furtive glancing and glowering at Angie while sipping black coffees. Ellie noticed them when she entered the shop to get some treats from the bakery case and as she passed by Angie she whispered a question about why they couldn't just get black coffee in their own kitchen instead of coming to the shop for it. Angie told Ellie that the couple's enjoyment came from scowling at her and muttering and not from indulging in the bakery offerings.

Just then, Betty Hayes, carrying a briefcase, bustled by on the sidewalk and passed the two people. Noticing the couple, she halted. Betty said something to them and Jenna watched the elderly couple huddle closer together, give a quick nod at the Realtor, and scurry away leaving Betty staring after them.

"Here comes Betty." Jenna watched the woman whirl, come around the corner of the building, and fly through the front door.

Betty almost dashed by the sisters, but she spotted them in the waiting area and hurried over with a questioning look. "Do we have a meeting?"

"We just stopped by." Angie stood up. "We wanted to talk to you for a minute."

"I barely have a second." Betty took off for her

office gesturing for the two Roselands to follow her. Inside the glass office space, she tossed her briefcase on the caramel-colored leather sofa and plopped down in her chair behind the desk where she started tapping on the laptop keyboard. "What do you want to talk about?"

Jenna gently closed the door and the girls took the two chairs in front of the desk.

Angie said, "We'd like to know the names of the couple who rented the Greenhill Road house from you."

Betty's fingers held suspended over the keyboard and she slowly raised her eyes to the sisters. "Why do I have a mental block on this?" She used her feet to push back in her chair and it rolled to the blonde wood credenza behind her. Betty pulled on one of the drawers and rustled through the files until she removed the one she wanted. She rolled back to the desk, slid her reading glasses on, and opened it. "Here it is. Clarence and Angelina Crosswort."

"Crosswort?" Jenna scrunched up her nose. "What a weird last name."

"They are weird people." Betty frowned.

"Where did they live before this?" Angie asked.

Betty sighed and returned to read from the sheet of paper in the file. She ran her finger down the paperwork. "Boston."

"Really? Where in Boston?" Angie and her sisters had grown up in the city.

"Yawkey Way. Number four." Betty closed the

folder.

A scurry of anxiety fluttered down Angie's back, but before she could say anything, Jenna asked, "Do you know how long they lived in Boston? Did they move around a lot or were they in the city most of their lives?"

"The file doesn't have that sort of information. They told me they had lived in Boston for years and had decided to move to the seacoast for a while. The couple was not forthcoming with any information. When I tried to make chitchat, they blew off any questions that I asked." Betty tapped her silver pen on the desktop for a few seconds. "I'm glad that transaction has been completed. I didn't like the couple. Believe me, I've had plenty of difficult clients, but these two were oddballs. They made me very wary and uneasy." She ran her hand over her eyes. "I don't really know why I felt that way. I suppose it was silly of me to feel so suspicious of them."

"I think you have good reason to be distrustful." Angie's face was serious and the tone of her voice made Jenna and Betty turn to her. "They lied about their address."

"What?" Betty flung open the folder and checked what she'd told the girls. "How do you know they lied? What's wrong with what they told me?"

"Four Yawkey Way? That's the address of Fenway Park."

Betty looked blank for a second.

"Fenway Park. The home of the Boston Red Sox." Angie's mind was racing. "And I know for sure that the Crossworts are not the owners of the Red Sox."

Betty's brow furrowed in anger. "Those two lousy...." She didn't finish the sentence, but the sisters knew pretty well what the Realtor probably wanted to say.

Jenna rolled her eyes. "I didn't pick up on the address. I wonder if they even gave you their real names. Maybe they lied about that, too."

"Oh, for heaven's sake." Betty tossed her pen down. "You can't trust anyone these days." Her phone buzzed, she took a look at the screen, and stood up. "I have a meeting." She gathered up a leather folder and headed for the office door. "If you see those two creeps around town, give them a piece of my mind." She stormed away leaving the girls still sitting in the seats in front of the desk.

***

HEADING HOME from the meeting with Betty, the girls took the longer way back to the Victorian so they could go past the Sweet Cove town common. Every October, the town put on a fall festival and part of the festivities involved a scarecrow contest.

"Look at all the scarecrows." Jenna smiled at the

different entries. "It must be a record year for entries."

Angie admired the variety of entries that ranged from scary to cute to imaginative. "We need to finish up our scarecrow and get him placed on the common by this weekend. I didn't realize so many people entered so early."

The girls strolled along pointing out the clever and original creations that they most enjoyed. The contest had different categories and was open to individuals, families, civic groups, and businesses. This year's theme was "Good Gourd" and each entry had to have at least one type of gourd incorporated into it. Many of the businesses in town made scarecrows related to their store or shop. The Pirate's Den restaurant had gone all out building a small replica of a sailing ship with two pirate-scarecrows, their heads made of pumpkins, on board the deck.

"We better up our game," Angie said eyeing the entries.

The town looked beautiful with the stores and homes decorated with carved pumpkins, fall flowers in pots or window boxes, and tiny sparkling white and orange lights strung over porch railings and around windows.

"I love fall." Some fallen red and yellow leaves crunched under Jenna's feet. "I love Halloween and the costumes and the crisp weather."

Angie chuckled and slipped her hand through

Jenna's arm. "I like it, too. The only thing is that it runs right into winter which is not my favorite time of year."

"You might like it this year though. Winter in a small town can be cozy and we aren't far from skiing areas. Maybe we can all take lessons."

Angie eyed her sister. "You forget I'm afraid of heights. Not sure I could ski down a mountain."

Dusk was falling when the two turned down the driveway of the Victorian and headed around to the back door. Courtney and Rufus Fudge had lit some logs in the fire pit and were sitting in the Adirondack chairs watching the flames. Jenna and Angie sat down across from them and held their cold hands up to the warm air coming off the fire. The four discussed how nice the center of town looked with all the decorations and scarecrows on the common.

"Ellie's bringing out some cookies and cupcakes and warm cider pretty soon. She told the B and B guests that there would be a fire and treats out here at 5:30. It was our job to get the fire going." Courtney stood up and went to the refreshment table situated under the pergola where she righted a pot of mums that had tipped over. The pergola was decorated with tiny white lights, cornstalks tied to each of the posts, and pumpkins arranged at the bottom of the stalks.

Rufus was leaning back on the chair and looking up at the darkening sky. Something in the old oak next to the carriage house caught his eye. "There's mistletoe growing in that tree."

Angie craned around to see. "Mistletoe? It grows around here?"

"It's right there." Rufus pointed. "On the higher branches. See? The greenery with the little, white berries. It's a parasitic plant that grows inside the branches and takes nutrients from the host tree."

"How do you know about mistletoe?" Jenna looked up at the branches that were illuminated by the security light on the carriage house roof.

"I took a class on mythology and fairytales as an undergraduate. Mistletoe is supposed to be magical. It's said to have healing properties and protects people from harm." Rufus smiled. "There are all kinds of legends around the plant. The French used to think that if someone held a sprig of mistletoe then they would be able to see ghosts and make them speak."

Jenna shifted uncomfortably in her seat and narrowed her eyes at the young man.

"You're making this up."

Rufus shook his head. "It's even supposed to ward off fires ...have the power to open all locks ... and light up the darkness."

"It is certainly an all-purpose plant." Angie laughed. "And I thought it was only a symbol of love."

"It's that, too." Rufus looked across the lawn to see Courtney approaching them.

"Well, I've heard that if a couple kisses while standing under mistletoe then they will always be together and will have a happy life." Jenna eyed Rufus and whispered. "Maybe you'd better kiss that pretty girl you have your eye on underneath the oak tree."

Rufus stood up, his eyes twinkling. "Oh, I intend to."

CHAPTER 6

Ellie carried a platter of homemade donuts to the table under the pergola and placed them next to a plate of caramel-oat-chocolate chip cookies. She'd made three different kinds of donuts, plain, apple-cinnamon, and powdered sugar. Ellie nudged Angie with her elbow and smiled proudly. "Try one of my donuts. I'm getting pretty good at the making treats thing."

Angie winked. "Maybe a making treats gene runs in the family."

Many of the B and B guests stood near the pergola or sat in the chairs around the fire pit mingling and chatting with one another. Several torches ringed the periphery of the garden lighting up the darkness. Angie stood near the treat table sipping some warm apple cider and admiring the pretty backyard. A sense of calm ran through her body, the recent unease she'd been feeling was momentarily forgotten as she enjoyed the chilly October evening.

Something at the rear window of the Victorian

caught her eye and she saw Euclid sitting on a table inside the sunroom staring at her through the glass. When Angie made eye contact with him, a flutter of worry gripped her chest.

Someone stepped next to Angie and the sudden appearance made her heart rate speed up. "Hello there," the man said. "It's Angie, correct?" Mr. Withers stood so close to Angie that he made her uncomfortable. She took a small step back.

Angie swallowed hard and nodded. "Hello, Mr. Withers."

"Call me Walter." He glanced at the drinks table. "Anything with a bit of alcohol in it?"

"There's wine and some craft beer."

"Huh." Withers gave a little snort. "I was hoping for something a little harder."

Angie took a quick glance over the man's shoulder to the window. Euclid had his back arched and his eyes glued to Withers.

"How are you enjoying your stay in Sweet Cove?" Angie wanted to get away from the man, but didn't want to appear rude so she forced herself to make some small talk.

Withers looked over the crowd gathered in the yard. "An interesting town."

"You mean because of its history?"

"What?" Withers asked distractedly.

"The history." Angie moved a little further away. "Do you enjoy the area's history?"

"Yes, very interesting." Withers eyed the garden

and the old oak tree.

Angie followed the man's gaze and realized that he seemed to be looking at the mistletoe growing in the branches of the oak. She shook herself thinking she was just imagining that Withers was eyeing the plant.

"Mistletoe, huh?" Withers mumbled.

Angie's eyes went wide. She didn't respond to the statement, just waited to see if the man would say anything else.

Mr. Finch, leaning on his cane, sidled up next to Withers and Angie. Angie had never been so happy to see him. "Nice evening, isn't it."

"Mr. Finch. Good to see you." Withers pumped Finch's hand with such vigor that Angie feared he might dislocate Mr. Finch's shoulder. "I haven't been into town today. I plan to make a stop at your award-winning candy shop before I leave the area."

Angie narrowed her eyes. How did Withers know that the candy store had won awards?

Mr. Finch said, "The store won its awards before Miss Courtney and I took it over."

"Really? I was sure the place was owned by you when the awards were given."

"You're mistaking me for my brother, Thaddeus Finch. He owned the store prior to my acquiring it."

"So candy-making runs in the family then." Withers clapped Finch on the shoulder. "Where'd your brother up and run off to? He retire?"

Mr. Finch's face was serious. "He was murdered."

Withers stammered for a few seconds. "So sorry. Wasn't expecting that. Someone unhappy with the product?"

Angie glared at the man for making such a ridiculous statement.

"The product was fine." Mr. Finch straightened. "My brother was not." He tapped his cane on the brick patio.

"Had a falling out?" Withers' dark eyes bored into Finch, his tone a bit too eager.

"So to speak." Finch moved to the treat table and chose an apple-cinnamon donut from the tray. "Miss Courtney and I have devised a new fudge flavor. We're calling it Apple Pie. I believe you will be impressed with the taste."

Angie grinned. "I'll come by tomorrow."

"I've never met a candy-maker before." Withers held a bottle of beer since hard liquor was unavailable at the small gathering. "Tell me about your background."

Finch swallowed a bite of donut. "I think we covered most of the interesting parts about me at dinner the other night. But we haven't had a chance to hear about you."

Angie jumped in. "Yes, tell us a bit about yourself, Mr. Withers."

"Call me Walter." He took a long swig from his beer bottle. "I'm afraid talking about myself would

46

just bore you to tears. There are a lot better topics to engage in."

"Nonsense." Mr Finch dusted the sugar from his fingertips. "Everyone's life is intriguing and unique. What does your work entail? Do you have your own business?"

"My work is very technical. No one understands it."

"Really?" Angie eyed him. "It can't be that difficult to understand. Can you explain it in general terms?"

"I'm afraid not."

"What are you? A secret agent?" Courtney came up and joined the group of three. "Do you work for the CIA or something?" She had a wide smile on her face.

Withers gave a chuckle. He said to Courtney, "I hear you and your partner, here, have come up with a new fudge flavor. I'm quite partial to fudge. I'll have to come by to give my opinion."

Angie and Finch exchanged a look acknowledging how deftly Withers moved the conversation to something other than himself.

"You don't like talking about yourself, Mr. Withers?" Courtney used a joking tone. "That can make people suspicious of you, you know."

"It's always best not to reveal too much." Withers started away. He winked. "Better to keep people guessing."

When he was on the other side of the yard and

out of ear-shot, Courtney frowned. "What an annoying man. If he doesn't want to reveal information about himself, then why doesn't he just make stuff up instead of causing people to wonder what he's hiding?"

"That would be the smarter thing to do." Angie watched Withers standing near the fire pit talking with some other B and B guests. "I think we'd better do our research on Mr. Withers."

"That's probably not even his real name." Courtney went to the treat table, lifted an empty platter, and turned to bring it inside to the kitchen.

Without warning, a sense of dread shot through Angie's body and shifting her gaze to the corner of the yard, she saw Police Chief Martin come around the house from the driveway. He stood looking about the crowd until he spotted Angie under the pergola with Mr. Finch and Courtney. Angie waved. Just one look at his face told her that something was wrong.

"Uh oh," Courtney said. "Here comes trouble."

"Indeed." Mr. Finch put both hands over the top of his cane and leaned heavily on it waiting for Chief Martin to cross the lawn.

"Evening." He nodded at the Roseland sisters and Mr. Finch. "I rang at the front door, but no one answered. I saw the lights back here and heard people talking so I came around."

Jenna and Ellie hurried over when they saw the chief.

48

"What's wrong now?" Ellie's voice trembled and she shoved her hands into the pockets of her light jacket.

"Some vandalism on the town common." The chief glanced around at the gathering. "The yard looks nice."

"Would you like something to drink?" Ellie gestured to the table of goodies. "Something to eat?"

The chief sighed. "No thanks."

Finch watched the chief's face. "Do you need us to help you with something?"

Chief Martin's jaw tightened. "I might." He shifted from foot to foot.

"What is it?" Jenna asked. "What kind of vandalism took place on the common? Did something happen to some of the scarecrows?"

The chief's eyes clouded as he looked from sister to sister and then at Finch. He cleared his throat. "Well, it has to do with you. All of you."

Angie breathed a sigh of relief. "It must be a mistake. We don't have a scarecrow entered in the contest yet so it can't be anything to do with us."

Chief Martin's face took on a pinched expression. "I'm afraid it does. Can you come with me or do you have to stay here with your guests?"

"You need all of us?" Ellie's voice went up an octave.

"I think all of you should come." The chief's eyes were dark and his lids were heavy.

"What about the cats?" Courtney questioned. "Should they come with us?"

The chief gave a quick nod. "The cats, too."

Angie's heart sank into a dark pool of dread.

CHAPTER 7

Ellie drove behind the chief's squad car until they reached the town common where she pulled up to the curb. The sisters, Finch, and the cats sat in the van and peered out over the common.

"I don't see anything wrong." Courtney sat staring through the windshield from the front passenger seat.

"Come on. Let's get it over with and see what Chief Martin wants to show us." Ellie sighed, opened her door, and slid out. The others did the same.

Walking to the chief's car, they could see a group of people congregated at the far end of the grass. In the darkness, the scarecrows seemed to menace the area, their forms making long shadows like monsters looming over the common. A burning smell lingered on the air. A fire truck was parked at the end of the common, its lights flashing off the trees and buildings.

Ellie grabbed Jenna's arm. "Everything feels wrong. You don't think there's a dead body, do you?"

"The chief would have warned us," Jenna reassured her sister. "He knows how you feel about such things."

The five people followed the chief with the cats trailing behind them. Angie took a look back at Euclid. The orange cat sniffed the air and scowled.

Chief Martin gestured ahead. "Someone called it in. They said there were flames on the common. It turns out that some scarecrows were set on fire."

Angie shuddered. "Why do you want us to see them?"

"Because." The chief didn't look at Angie. "I think there's a message in what was done."

Angie couldn't keep a groan from escaping from her throat. As they approached the scene, their feet scrunched over the fallen leaves and a sudden breeze sent them swirling into the air. Several officers stood guard by the burned forms and police tape had been strung around the spot.

Courtney held Mr. Finch's arm so he wouldn't stumble on the uneven ground. When she saw what was ahead, she sucked in her breath. "Oh."

Five simple, singed scarecrows stood side-by-side with two small forms shaped like cats positioned at their feet. A ring of small piles of hay surrounded the scarecrows and had been set aflame in order to call attention to the creations, but keep them from catching fire and burning up.

"Those scarecrows are supposed to be us."

Courtney scowled, anger flaming in her eyes.

Ellie covered her mouth with her hand and spun around to face in the other direction.

Jenna took a step forward. "What's it supposed to mean?" She turned to the chief. "Is it a warning of some sort? Do you think it's a harmless act or are we in danger?"

"Do you sense anything?" Chief Martin asked quietly.

"May we walk around the scene?" Mr. Finch asked Jenna. She nodded and the two set off side-by-side to check the scarecrows from the other side.

"Why would someone do this?" Angie tilted her head, her eyes moving over the charred piles of hay and the singed forms.

"We haven't had a run-in with anyone." Ellie spoke with her back to the scene.

"Not lately, anyway," Courtney glanced down. "Where are the cats?"

Everyone looked about the common trying to see where the animals had gone. Lights reflected off of Euclid's orange and white plume and they detected him almost immediately. He was sniffing around the scarecrow cats.

"There's Euclid." The chief pointed. "But where's Circe?"

"She must be near the scarecrows, too." Courtney started to duck under the police tape. "Can we go in?"

The chief nodded and lifted the tape up so the

girls could enter the cordoned off space.

"Can I stay here?" Ellie didn't want anything to do with the problem.

"Sure," Courtney told her. "But watch out for the boogie-man."

Ellie shuddered and stayed put where she had planted herself. "Hurry up, okay?"

Walking around the odd scene, they met up with Jenna and Mr. Finch and found their black cat sniffing around with Euclid.

"We're hoping its just kids playing a stupid prank," Jenna said as she came alongside Angie and the chief. She shrugged a shoulder and made a face indicating that she and Mr. Finch figured it was probably something more.

"That's what I'm hoping as well." The chief watched one of his officers taking photos of the area.

Angie heard the hesitation in his voice. "But what? You think it's something else?"

"It's pretty elaborate. Who would go to all this trouble? Putting together five human scarecrows and the two cats? Setting up the fire so it would bring the fire department, but wouldn't burn down the scarecrows. It's a lot of work for a prank."

"It's pretty clear that there's a message in this mess." Courtney walked another loop around the area.

The chief turned. "I don't like it. I see it as a warning to all of you. But who did it and why, are the questions." He rubbed his forehead. "I wonder if it's someone involved in recent cases you've helped out on."

Jenna narrowed her eyes in thought. "We should make a list of the cases, who was involved, and who might want revenge on us for bringing someone to justice."

Angie looked about the common. "Do any of the businesses around here have security cameras that might have caught the action of whoever did this?"

"A couple of the officers are looking into that right now." The chief glanced about the street. "People who were around at the time the scarecrows were probably being set up are being questioned about whether they saw anything. We won't have any information until tomorrow at the earliest." He took his hat off, smoothed his hair, and placed the cap back on his head. "I need to go talk to my men. Walk around some more, if you want. Let's meet tomorrow and share thoughts." The chief started away. "Thanks for coming out. I thought you should see it."

Angie nodded. "Give us a call. We'll do some thinking."

Ellie took a peek at her sisters. "Can we leave?"

"I think we should try to pick up on anything, you know, floating on the air," Jenna suggested.

"You can wait in the van if you've had enough," Angie told Ellie sympathetically. "We won't be long."

"Try not to be. I want to get home." Ellie headed for her vehicle, her long blonde hair swinging over her back as she hurried away.

The girls, cats, and Mr. Finch stood quietly here and there near the police tape, each one trying to get a sense of what happened and why. Angie closed her eyes for a few moments trying to clear her mind. She took deep breaths in and out and the smell of the burnt material suddenly tickled her nose. Courtney bent down and picked up some of the burned remnants of hay and she handed it to Mr. Finch. Jenna sat down on the damp grass and stared at the shadowy forms trying to sense the person who created the scarecrows. The cats continued to gingerly snoop around the objects, sniffing and pawing.

"Do you sense anything, Mr. Finch?" Courtney came up beside the man.

"The person was clever. Whoever was involved with this was wearing gloves so I am unable to pick up on much." Finch lifted the hay to his nose and inhaled. "I get a whiff of an accelerant like lighter fluid or gasoline, but it's faint."

Angie reported to them that when she was concentrating on the scene she'd gotten a whiff of gasoline as well. "It's funny though. I didn't smell any of that when we were walking around and I don't smell it now.

"We should ask Chief Martin if an accelerant was used to start the fires." Courtney inhaled a deep breath. "I don't smell anything other than that burnt odor."

Angie noticed Professor Tyler, the researcher and new B and B guest standing with a group of people at the edge of the common and she walked over to speak with him.

"A strange bit of mischief." Professor Tyler was dressed in a dark raincoat. "But it's the season for mischief, isn't it?"

Angie nodded. "I wonder if it was kids."

"Most likely it was some teenagers looking to scare the townspeople with their silly prank. I was out to dinner and saw the crowd here as I was walking around." Tyler adjusted his blue and red scarf against the evening chill.

Angie's eyes widened. "Did you happen to notice anyone on the common who might have been up to no good?"

"I'm afraid I didn't. I just got here really. I heard people talking about what happened." The man shrugged. "It's nothing to be concerned over, just a Halloween prank."

Jenna waved to her sister and Angie nodded to her. She wished Professor Tyler a good evening. "See you at the B and B."

When she returned to her family, Finch asked, "Shall we go back to the van? Miss Ellie will be getting nervous."

"I think we're done here. Here come the cats." Angie noticed that Circe was carrying something in her mouth as she walked towards them with Euclid by her side. Angie knelt on one knee. "What do you have, little one?"

Circe dropped the thing onto the lawn and Angie reached for it. "It's a piece of a plant." She handed it to Mr. Finch.

"How odd." Finch examined the sprig. "Mistletoe."

***

ELLIE SAT in the driver's seat of the van. She had her arms wrapped around herself and her heart was pounding. She almost wished she had stayed at the other end of the common with her family. The van was parked under a large Maple tree and its bare branches hung over the vehicle like arms reaching out to grab anyone moving past. Ellie knew her imagination was running away with her and she tried to focus on something pleasant to distract her thoughts from the vandalism and its seeming intended threat.

She closed her eyes and pictured Jack. She smiled at the image of the young attorney and his ever-present bow tie. As Ellie was thinking how nice it would be to have Jack sitting right next to her, a sense of fear raced through her body causing her to shoot up straighter in her seat. Her head whipped around from side to side so she could look out all of the van's windows. Seeing her sisters, the cats, and Mr. Finch approaching from the far end of the common, she leaned back with a sigh brushing off her flash of anxiety.

Trying to calm her breathing, she glanced out the through the windshield and saw a figure standing at the corner of the street ahead of her. The figure was in shadow, but she could see it was wearing a long dark coat that reached nearly to the ankles. The hood was pulled up over the head. Ellie could see that the figure was watching her family walking towards the van. The person took a step as if it was about to move away down the street, but then it paused and the shadow-covered face turned slowly towards Ellie.

For a long second, Ellie felt the figure's eyes bore into her and a shudder of ice cold fear ran through her core. The figure whirled, rushed down the street, and was gone.

CHAPTER 8

Angie and Jenna headed down Main Street to the Sweet Cove Police Department. Chief Martin stopped in at the bake shop early that morning and asked if the Roselands and Mr. Finch might come by in the afternoon to sit in on an interview with a person claiming to have seen a man on the common last night. Finch and Courtney couldn't go along because two employees called in sick and they both had to work at the candy store. Ellie had no interest in being present at the interview so she promised to watch Jenna's jewelry shop while her older sisters went to see the chief.

The witness hadn't shown up yet so Angie and Jenna sat with Chief Martin to get an update.

"Last night a man at the scene reported that his wife had been walking their dog around the center of town. On her way back, flames were burning on the common. She called her husband and he went up to meet her to see what was going on. She told him that she'd seen someone putting up new scarecrows as she walked past and on her way

home the flames were burning. The wife stayed with her husband for a few minutes watching the hubbub on the common and then she left and went home before officers arrived so no one spoke with her last night. She should be here any minute." The chief glanced at his watch. "She's fifteen minutes late."

"Maybe she changed her mind about coming." Jenna wondered if the woman got spooked by the prior evening's activities and decided not to talk about it.

Angie tapped her finger on the table as she thought about the strange happenings on the common. "Was there any evidence of accelerant used to start the fires?

"Not to my knowledge, but all the data isn't in yet. The fire chief hasn't called today. I'll ask him about it." Chief Martin gave Angie a questioning look.

"Last night when the four of us were standing quietly trying to pick up on anything, Mr. Finch and I got the sensation that we could smell something like gasoline or lighter fluid. It was odd though since none of us could smell anything like that when we'd been walking around the scene."

"I'll call the fire chief after our meeting." The chief made a note on his pad of paper.

A knock sounded at the door of the conference room and an officer ushered in a woman who appeared to be in her early sixties. She had short blonde hair and looked slim and athletic. Little worry lines creased the corners of her eyes and she took quick glances at the three people in the room. The girls and the chief stood and made introductions.

The woman sat, her face screwed up with worry. "You don't suspect *me* for setting that fire, do you?"

"Not at all." Chief Martin sat across from her. "We're just gathering information."

The woman eyed Angie with a quizzical expression. "You own the bake shop."

Angie nodded and the chief jumped in with an explanation. "Miss Roseland has some experience with investigation."

The woman appeared to accept the comment and after a few preliminary questions from the chief, Mrs. Margaret Sullivan recounted what she'd seen last night which mirrored what her husband had reported to the police.

"It was a lovely night. Dark though. I took the dog on our usual evening walk through town. The common looked great with all the scarecrows set up. On our way back, I smelled smoke and when we got closer I could see the flames." Mrs. Sullivan clutched her hands together and placed them on the tabletop.

"How busy was it around town last night?" The chief used a calm, friendly tone which seemed to help put the woman at ease.

"The center of town always has some activity

going on even in the winter." The woman brushed at her bangs. "Not as much as summer of course, but people are out walking around or going out to a restaurant. The fall is a lovely time of year in Sweet Cove. I never feel worried when I go out at night even when I'm alone. I feel safe."

Angie wondered if the woman had heard about the murders and odd happenings that had gone on in town the past spring and summer. It was enough to make anyone have at least a passing concern. Maybe Mrs. Sullivan believed bad things only happened to bad people.

"And last night? Were people around?" the chief asked.

The woman nodded. "Sure. There were people strolling on the sidewalks. I noticed a few folks on the common admiring the scarecrows."

"You saw someone putting up new scarecrows?" The chief encouraged Mrs. Sullivan with a nod.

"I did. A man was pushing the posts into the ground. You know, the end of the scarecrow has a sharp post so it can be secured into the ground. I was at the other side of the common. I wondered if there might be something else to go along with the scarecrows, you know, like the display of the pirate ship that's set up there."

"What made you wonder that?" Jenna gave a sweet smile to the woman.

"Well, because the things the man was putting in the ground didn't compare to the other entries."

"How so?" Angie asked.

"The ones he had were, well, crude. No effort had gone into making costumes for them or anything. They were just stick figures, really. I made a mental note to myself to see how they looked up closer as I passed by on the way home."

"What about the man who was setting up the new scarecrows?" Chief Martin was writing on a pad of paper. "Did he look familiar? How would you describe him?"

Mrs. Sullivan's forehead scrunched up. "Hmm. I was so interested in the new display he was erecting that I didn't pay much attention to him."

"What was he wearing?"

"It was dark, I couldn't see much. A wool coat, I think. Dark pants. Gloves. Maybe a baseball hat."

"Could you estimate his age?"

The woman bit her lower lip. "I wouldn't say young, maybe middle aged or older?"

Angie groaned inwardly at the lack of details. "Was there a vehicle? Was he going back and forth to a truck or a car?"

"I didn't notice a vehicle. He was just working on the set-up. I didn't see him go to a truck or anything." Mrs. Sullivan frowned. "I'm not much help, I'm afraid."

"Every bit of information is helpful." Chief Martin gave a reassuring nod and smile. "Can you tell us what you saw on the way home?"

"The dog and I walked our usual side streets and

64

then we headed back to the common. I could smell burning. At first, I thought someone might have a wood stove going and that's what I could smell, but getting closer, the odor was strong and heavy. I picked up my pace and when I got near the common I saw the flames. I called my husband to tell him what was going on." Mrs. Sullivan clenched and unclenched her hands. "I got worried the fire might spread to the buildings and stores in the town center."

"On your way back, did you see the man who had put up the new scarecrows? Was he still there?" Angie leaned forward.

"He might have been, but I was so intent on the fire that I didn't notice if the man was still around or not."

Chief Martin asked, "What happened then?"

"I stood with some people. We were talking about what could have happened. The fire truck came. Police cars showed up. My husband came to see what was going on."

"You stayed for a while?" Jenna questioned.

"I didn't stay for very long after my husband arrived. The dog was fussing and pulling on the leash. All the commotion was making him upset so I decided to take him home."

"Did you notice anything else?" Chief Martin rested his pen on the pad of paper. "Anything that seemed slightly off or odd. Anything at all that caught your eye."

Mrs. Sullivan thought for a few moments. Her lips turned down. "Just the oddness of the scene. The fire burning around the five scarecrows. It was disturbing, I must say. It almost seemed like some old pagan ceremony or a sacrifice or something. It gave me a chill." She unclasped her hands and waved one of them about. "My husband and I discussed it. We decided kids must have done it. You know how teenagers can get into mischief. That's all it is. Nothing to worry about."

"Did you notice any teenagers around?" Jenna's blue eyes were warm and friendly. She hoped the woman might recall seeing some kids milling about enjoying the commotion that their actions caused ... if the cause was indeed kids pulling a prank.

"I can't say if any teens were nearby or not. I didn't notice. No one stood out." She raised her hands in a gesture of helplessness. "Well, one person stood out, but not for any reasons having to do with the fire." Mrs. Sullivan shook her head.

"What do you mean?" Angie tilted her head in a questioning posture.

"Someone was standing on the corner watching the fire. I don't know if it was a man or a woman. The person had on a long coat, almost all the way down to the ankles. It was very unflattering. It even had a hood pulled up." Mrs. Sullivan tsk-tsked. "Why anyone would wear such a coat is beyond me. Frankly, I can only describe it as ugly."

Angie and Jenna eyed each other with concern.

Mrs. Sullivan was describing the very same person Ellie had seen last night while she was sitting in her van. The person who had been watching them.

CHAPTER 9

The interview ended and Chief Martin went to place a call to the fire chief to ask about accelerants. He promised to text Angie if there was any news.

Angie held the door of the police station open for Jenna. "Who is this person in the long coat? Why is he ... or she, watching us?"

Jenna zipped up her sweater and stepped out into the chill of the overcast day. "Maybe the person wasn't watching us with any ill intent. There was a fire. He came out to see what was going on. Maybe he was watching the excitement and wasn't really focusing on us at all. He could have been just looking in our direction."

Angie stopped walking and faced her twin sister. "He looked at Ellie. His look scared her."

"Ellie can be...." Jenna gave a little shrug of one shoulder. "You know."

Angie started down the sidewalk with a sigh. "It worries me. Ellie isn't usually wrong about people."

"She could have overblown it though. She was rattled about the scarecrows. She wasn't that close to him, she couldn't really see his face. Maybe she let her emotions get away from her."

"That could be." Angie wasn't convinced though. Despite being jittery when Ellie helped on cases, she hardly ever picked up the wrong emotion or intention from a person. "Want to walk by the common? Check out the scene again?"

"Sure." The girls walked in step along the cozy streets of Sweet Cove heading to the center of town. "Mrs. Sullivan didn't give us a whole lot of information. The most interesting part was the guy in the coat." Jenna admired the red and orange leaves on the branches of the trees and then something about the fire came into her mind that caused her to frown. "Suppose this fire thing really was meant as a warning message to us." She pushed her hair back over her shoulder. "Then what in the world is the message?"

"That's puzzling," Angie pondered. "If someone wanted to hurt us then why send a message at all? Why not just go ahead and try to harm us?"

Jenna scowled. "Unless the person wants to unnerve us first. He might get a kick out of mentally torturing us before he makes an attempt to harm."

"Why target *us* though?" Angie nodded at a couple who passed by them. She glanced at her sister. "Have you had any more feelings that someone has been watching you when you're alone working on your house?"

Jenna kicked at some leaves on the sidewalk. "No. I've been bringing the cats with me." She looked at Angie with worried eyes. "You think the sensation I had of being watched when I was at the house is linked to the fire on the common?"

Angie scrunched her upper lip. "Maybe?"

Jenna groaned. "I love the house. Tom loves the house. We want to make it our home. It can't be ruined by some nut who wants to threaten us or send us cryptic fire messages." She squared her shoulders. "I won't let anyone ruin Tom's and my plans to live in that house together someday."

Angie gave a nod. "I didn't like what Mrs. Sullivan said about pagan ceremonies and sacrifices." A chill shivered down her spine and it wasn't because of the cool October air. "I hadn't thought of those things. Someone is sure trying to tell us something with those burning scarecrows."

The girls turned onto the main street of town and headed to the common. A good number of people were hurrying about doing errands, sightseeing in town, strolling by stores or walking to restaurants. A few people stood at the far end of the common looking over the burned grass and the spots were the scarecrows had been set. They had been cleared away leaving behind singed lawn and bits of the hay they had been stuffed with. The girls stood where the forms had been pushed into the grass and they stared at the spot without speaking.

Jenna finally broke the silence. "Circe found

some mistletoe here. Don't you find that odd?"

"Yup, I do. I've been trying to figure out how that plant figures into all of this. Rufus spotted it in the oak tree yesterday and an hour later Mr. Withers saw it and commented on it. Then last night Circe found a sprig of the plant on the common and brought it to me." Angie folded her arms over her chest. "It's odd for sure."

Jenna looked her sister in the eye. "Is the mistletoe part of the message?"

"Come on." Angie tugged on Jenna's arm. "Let's go to the candy store and talk everything over with Courtney and Mr. Finch. We need more brainpower on this."

***

THE CANDY store was abuzz with customers peering into the glass cases and pointing to the treats they wanted. Courtney and two employees greeted patrons, boxed goodies, and rang up the sales. Courtney's eyes narrowed when she saw her two sisters open the door and step into the shop. She handed a candy bag and some change to an older couple and then stepped out from behind the counter. She led Angie and Jenna into the back room where Mr. Finch was working on a batch of fudge.

Angie closed her eyes and inhaled deeply. "Heavenly." She looked at Mr. Finch. "Is the fudge ready?"

Finch used a metal spatula to smooth the top of the candy. "Are you hungry, Miss Angie?"

"I'm always hungry when I come in here." She leaned over Mr. Finch's shoulder. "Is this the new flavor? The apple pie fudge?"

"That one is in the fridge." Finch placed the spatula on the marble counter and straightened up. He reached for his cane. "I thought you might be stopping in. Shall I pour lattes?" He walked to his drink machine and pushed some buttons placing small white cups under the spout.

Courtney pulled up chairs. "How did the interview at the police station go?"

"That's what we want to talk to you about." Angie carried two cups to the small table Courtney had put in the middle of the chairs.

When the four were settled in the seats with their drinks, the girls reported to Courtney and Finch what Mrs. Sullivan had told them and then they voiced some of their worries and concerns.

"My first question is why are we being targeted?" Jenna sipped her latte. "If we can figure that out, we might be able to come up with a suspect."

"That might be difficult to determine, Miss Jenna. It could be anyone, really. It could be someone we know from town, someone who is related to a former case, or someone we've never met at all."

Jenna blew out a sigh. "I see what you mean."

Courtney said, "Is there something particular going on that might have drawn someone to want to bother us?"

"Like what? What do you mean?" Angie placed her cup on the table.

"What's going on with all of us? Is it because Jenna and Tom bought that house? Is it because Angie reopened the bake shop? Nothing's really new with Mr. Finch or me." Courtney looked from person to person. "Nothing's different for Ellie either except new guests at the B and B."

"That new guest, Mr. Withers is kind of mysterious." Jenna's lips turned down.

"And weird." Courtney harrumphed. "He can't tell us what his occupation is. He can't tell us where he lives or where he grew up. Like I've said a hundred times, why doesn't he just make stuff up to appease people when they try to make conversation. Then no one would be suspicious of him."

"He asks Ellie questions about us and he seems interested in our house, but doesn't say why." Jenna's annoyance and confusion about Withers and what he might want from her and Tom and her sisters was evident on her face.

"You had the feeling someone was watching you the other day when you were at the house." Courtney's comment made Jenna shift uneasily in her chair. "It might be the same person who set the fire."

"Something else that's new is that old couple who comes into the bake shop and glares at me." Angie reminded everyone how the couple lied to Betty Hayes about their former address in Boston.

"And the cats." Mr. Finch rubbed his palm over the top of his cane. "They were agitated the other day and tried as hard as they could to get into the bake shop. I don't believe I've ever seen them so determined." Finch thought about the past few months and how the cats had been instrumental in solving many cases. He modified his statement. "Well, thinking back on things, the cats *have* previously been as agitated as they were the other day, but this time was similar. Which doesn't bode well."

"They know trouble is brewing." Courtney shifted her attention to Finch. "After you held the wine bottle with Withers at dinner the other night you said that a whole heap of trouble is heading our way."

Finch gave a grave nod. "The cats and I sense it, but what *it* is has yet to reveal itself."

Angie clutched her hands in her lap. "Until things become clearer, we all need to keep on guard. We probably shouldn't be alone anywhere."

Jenna groaned, thinking of all the work that needed to be done on the house. She and Tom's free time didn't overlap often so they each went to the house to work when their schedules allowed.

Angie understood her sister's groan. "We should

at least let one of us know where we're going, when we get there, and when we're expected home. We need to keep tabs on each other."

Courtney went to the desk and took paper and pen out of the drawer. "You know how I love making lists." Her eyes twinkled. "Let's write down some suspects who might be trying to frighten us with burning scarecrows." She sat and wrote on the paper. "Weird Withers." She looked up with a smile. "That's his new name."

"The creepy couple who come into my shop almost every morning, the Crossworts," Angie said.

"Great. Creepy Crosswort Couple." Courtney wrote them down. "Every suspect has to have alliteration in their name or they don't get on the list," she joked.

Courtney could be counted on to lighten the mood and Angie loved that about her.

Angie said, "Here's another suspect. The person in the long coat who was watching the common last night."

Courtney cocked her head with the pen poised in the air. "Alliteration, please."

Angie stared at her youngest sister. "I'll work on that. Just write it down for now."

"I'll write Mysteriously-clothed Monitor for now." Courtney grinned. "Mr. Finch? Any suspects to add?"

Finch looked at each girl, his face slightly pale. "I was just thinking. I wonder." He swallowed.

"Could the coming danger have something to do with your Nana?"

The girls stared at Finch with wide eyes and Angie's heart sank.

CHAPTER 10

Nana? What do you mean?" Jenna's eyes widened. "How could the trouble have anything to do with Nana? She's been gone for years."

"I don't specifically mean that your Nana is involved." Mr. Finch looked over the tops of his glasses. "But I wonder if someone who knew your Nana has heard that her descendants are in Sweet Cove and doesn't like it." He held each sister's eyes. "Halloween is an excellent time to come to town. There are lots of people here, the costumes, the parties, the town festival. All good ways to blend in and do mischief."

"But if someone was out to harm us because of Nana, *you* wouldn't be a target." Courtney leaned forward.

"That's right." Angie looked at Mr. Finch. "You wouldn't be in danger if it had to do with Nana since you aren't a relative, but when you had the sensation of doom you felt it surrounded you as well, so it mustn't have anything to do with her."

Mr. Finch was quiet for a minute and when he

finally spoke, his voice was soft. "You are my family now. Harm will come to you over my dead body. If anyone means to hurt you, then I am in danger, too."

A smile crept over Courtney's lips. "I know nothing will ever happen to us while you're around, Mr. Finch."

Jenna turned to Finch. "And nothing will happen to *you* while we're around."

Angie's stomach was in a knot. "Why would someone not like that we're living in Sweet Cove now? Do you think Nana had an enemy?"

"From what you've told me, your Nana helped the police much the same way that we do." Finch's bushy eyebrows knitted together. "Your Nana's skills were probably well-developed and powerful. She most likely helped solve many cases which might mean she acquired some enemies." Mr. Finch stood up and went to the counter to check the fudge. He removed a pan from the cooler and started to cut it. "Perhaps someone from her past wants revenge or doesn't want her granddaughters picking up where she left off."

Something about what Finch was saying picked at Angie, but she couldn't understand what she was feeling. Jenna noticed the expression on her twin sister's face. "You think there's something to what Mr. Finch is saying?"

Angie blinked. She thought for a few moments. "Maybe?" She shifted her eyes to the older man. "A sense of foreboding washed over me when you mentioned an enemy. I don't know why or what it could mean."

"We need to do something, not just sit around waiting for a nut to attack us." Courtney tapped the pen against her chin. "Let's look up Mr. Withers on the internet tonight, see what we can find out about him."

Angie said, "I'll talk to Chief Martin about Nana and see if he has any insight."

"We should head home. It's getting dark." Jenna picked up her latte cup and carried it to the sink. "I've left Ellie in charge of the jewelry shop too long already. We can do some internet sleuthing after dinner."

Courtney looked at Angie. "Have you ever spoken to the creepy couple who comes into the bake shop?"

Angie's eyes widened. "No. They seem to hate me so I haven't spoken to them. I've tried smiling at them, but they look away and scowl. I really don't want anything to do with them."

"Well, you're about to get to know them." Courtney gave her sister a wicked grin. "I think one of your sleuthing assignments should be to talk to that couple when they come into the bake shop tomorrow morning."

Angie groaned and was about to protest.

"Honestly, I think that's a good idea." Jenna nodded. "Talk to them, throw them off guard. Chat with them, be friendly. Try to find out what they're up to."

Angie slowly shook her head. "I'll talk to them on one condition."

All eyes turned to her.

"You give me a giant square of that fudge to try." She smiled and the others chuckled.

Mr. Finch carried a piece of the new flavored fudge to the honey-blonde baker and she accepted it eagerly.

"Give us your honest opinion, Sis." Courtney waited for the verdict as her sister bit into the golden colored square.

Angie moaned and closed her eyes. "How did you do it? I taste apples, cinnamon, and pie pastry, too." Her eyes popped open. "How did you combine all those flavors together into the one pan of fudge?"

Courtney grinned, turned, and high-fived Mr. Finch.

"Tell me." Angie licked her finger.

"Nope." Courtney picked up the knife and started to cut the squares.

"But I'm your sister," Angie said. "You can tell me."

Courtney winked at Mr. Finch and looked over her shoulder at Angie. "We can't tell. It's a secret."

Just as Angie was about to try and persuade her sister or Mr. Finch to share their fudge secret, an employee came to the doorway. "Courtney?"

Courtney wiped her fingers on her apron realizing that she'd been away from the front of the shop for quite a while leaving the two employees to handle the customers on their own. "Sorry, Maddie, I'm coming out to help."

Maddie shook her head. "It's not that. Someone just came in and said there's a big fire in town. A house is burning down. It's pretty bad, I guess."

Courtney's jaw dropped and her sisters and Mr. Finch froze in place.

"Where?" Jenna's voice was shaky. "Did they say where it was?"

"Greenhill Road." Maddie went back to the front of the store.

"The Crosswort couple just signed a rental agreement on a house on Greenhill Road," Angie reminded them.

Jenna moved to Angie's side. "Another fire? What's going on?"

"That's a very good question." Angie eyed her sisters and Mr. Finch. "Let's go find out."

***

ELLIE PICKED up her sisters and Mr. Finch from in front of the store after receiving their call and she drove the van along the streets of town heading for Greenhill Road. Her passengers brought her up to speed about the interview at the police station and about their thoughts and worries

81

about the fire on the common.

"Was Weird Withers at the B and B this evening or has he been out?" Courtney immediately thought of him as a suspect in the house fire.

"I'm not sure." Ellie turned the steering wheel to head the van onto Greenhill Road. "I saw him after you left the house. He followed me around for a while yammering away at me. He said he had plans to visit the art museum today. I haven't seen him since early afternoon."

Courtney made an "aha" noise.

Jenna said, "Don't focus solely on Withers. If we only concentrate on him, we might overlook an important piece of evidence that points to someone else. Just because Withers went out today doesn't mean he's the fire bug."

"There are police ahead blocking the way." Ellie parked the van at the side of the road. "We'll have to walk from here."

Two police officers stood in front of orange cones that had been placed in a line across the road. A police car was parked diagonally on the street, its blue lights flashing. When the Roselands and Finch emerged from the van, one of the officers approached to tell them they couldn't park there. It was Officer Talbot and when he recognized the group, he waved them forward and told them he would radio Chief Martin to let him know they were on their way down to the scene.

The acrid smell of smoke stung their nostrils as

they rounded a bend in the street and got closer to the burning house.

"Oh, how awful." Ellie gasped and placed the palm of her hand against her cheek when she spotted the uproar ahead of them.

Flames could be seen shooting out of two downstairs windows. Three fire trucks were parked in the road and some firefighters held hoses and others hurried back and forth across the front lawn. Police walkie talkies and car radios crackled and squawked in the air. People stood across the street watching the goings-on and the sisters and Mr. Finch walked over to join the crowd. They recognized acquaintances and questioned them about what had happened.

A regular customer at the bake shop gave an account. "It took a long time to get the fire under control. The flames were coming out of the roof and the upstairs windows. It seems to be quieting down now."

"Was anyone inside?" Finch questioned.

"No one knows if anyone's in there," another bystander offered. "We haven't seen them take anyone out yet."

"Do you know who owns the house?" Jenna asked.

A young guy spoke up. "Some people named Johnson. They rent the place out by the week in the summer and then by the month for the rest of the year. The house has been empty for about two weeks since the last rental left. If the place doesn't get rented in the off-season then it usually gets winterized around this time. I live a few houses up the street." The guy pointed.

Angie leaned towards Mr. Finch. "I'm going to text Betty and ask the address of the house that the Crosswort couple recently rented from her." She pulled out her phone and sent the message. "I hope she answers before we leave."

The five of them stood quietly in the darkness taking in the scene, looking around at the people gathered on both sides of the street and at the neighboring houses. The flames had died down now and the sense of urgency was slowly dissipating.

"I don't think we should approach Chief Martin," Jenna said. "He looks much too busy."

Angie agreed. "We can talk to him tomorrow to find out if there's any link between the house fire and the fire on the common last night."

With a worried look on her face, Ellie shuffled from foot to foot in the chilly air. "Do you think someone set it?" She stared at the ruined house.

"It's possible." Mr. Finch leaned on his cane. "It could also have been something other than arson, an electrical issue, a gas leak."

Ellie fiddled with the ends of her long blonde hair. "I hope it was just some functional thing gone wrong."

Courtney grunted. "Kind of a coincidence that

we have two fires in two days in our sweet little town." She crossed her arms over her chest. "I'm leaning towards arson."

Ellie's voice quavered when she asked, "Can we go home now?"

They all agreed that there probably wasn't much else to see and as they turned to leave, they bumped into Francine from the stained glass shop. Francine had been helpful in providing some important information in the last case the Roselands had been involved with.

"Some unexpected trouble in town, huh?" Francine frowned as she watched the officials working in front of the burnt-out home. "I hope they get to the bottom of all this."

"You think it was set?" Jenna asked.

Francine gave a shrug. "I hope not, but I'm keeping every outside light burning around my house and shop just in case there's an arsonist on the loose. Maybe the nut will bypass my place if it's all lit up. It might make it harder for someone to sneak around. Did I tell you I'm moving my stained glass shop into the center of Sweet Cove?" She looked at Courtney and Mr. Finch. "I need a bigger space and I've leased the storefront four doors down from your candy store. Drop by sometime. I'm in there almost every day getting it ready."

While they were discussing the scarecrow fire on the town common, Angie's phone buzzed in her pocket. A text from Betty gave her the address of the Crossworts' recent rental. Angie glanced at the number engraved in the granite post supporting the mailbox for the house they were standing in front of and realized it was one number off from the Crossworts' house. Looking across the street, she squinted at the mailbox post and her heart skipped a beat. The house the Crossworts had just rented stood right next door to the house that was on fire.

The Crosswort home was shrouded in darkness. Angie shifted her gaze from window to window starting with the second floor and just when she lowered her eyes to scan the first floor she had the sensation of something passing behind the glass of one of the upper windows. As she was turning her attention back to the second floor, something caught her eye on the sidewalk three houses up from the fire.

A figure, wearing a long dark poncho with the hood up, stood on the sidewalk watching the fire fighters. Angie's throat constricted. She took a step towards the figure just as the person turned and began to hurry away up the road.

"I'll be right back." Angie sprinted up the dark street following the hooded form and when she was right behind it, she reached out her hand and touched it on the shoulder.

The figure stopped so suddenly that the cessation of forward movement caused the poncho's fabric to swirl around its ankles. The person spun on its heel and stood face to face with

Angie.

CHAPTER 11

In a split second, the hooded person's expression transformed from annoyance and concern to friendly recognition. "Angie. You scared me."

Angie blinked. "Gloria. What are you doing here?"

The sixty-something blonde woman smiled. "I live a couple of blocks away. I was walking home from the salon and someone told me there was a fire in my neighborhood. I scooted over here. You startled me." The woman chuckled. "You're lucky I didn't pepper spray you." Angie had been going to Gloria for hair cutting ever since she'd moved to Sweet Cove. Gloria eyed Angie. "You okay?"

"Yeah." Angie forced a smile. "I thought you were someone else. I thought I recognized your shawl."

Gloria ran her hand down the front of her garment. "It's a poncho actually. I've never worn one, but when I tried it on at the store, I decided that I had to have it. It's so comfortable, and keeps me so warm. It's been cold out at night." She looked at Angie, her eyes serious. "You don't think I'm too old to wear something like this, do you?"

Angie was so surprised to see her hair stylist on the street in the long overcoat that she had to give herself a little shake. "No, of course not."

"You sure?" Gloria glanced down at her ankles. "Does the length make me look even shorter?"

"You look great." Angie smiled. "You shouldn't be asking me for fashion advice. I should be asking you." Gloria always had her hair and makeup done perfectly and she wore stylish and well-tailored outfits. Angie was feeling foolish for rushing up on the woman in the dark. They discussed the house fire and the scarecrow fire on the common.

"Were you at the common last night?" Angie asked, wondering if Gloria was the person that Ellie had seen standing on the dark street corner last evening.

"No." Gloria shook her head causing the hood of the poncho to slip down onto her shoulders. "I was in West Cove visiting a friend. Did you see the fire?"

Angie told the woman that she and her sisters had gone over to the common after hearing about what was going on, but by the time they got there, the fire was out.

"It's worrying." Gloria's eyes darkened. "I hope they hurry up and catch whoever's setting these fires before someone gets hurt."

Angie's sisters and Mr. Finch came up. They

greeted the friendly hair stylist and chatted about the concerning events going on in town. Gloria said, "I better get going. Bob must be wondering why I'm not home yet." She gave the others a smile and headed off up the street.

"I thought maybe Gloria was the suspicious person in the dark coat you saw last night," Angie told Ellie. "But she wasn't in Sweet Cove. She was in West Cove last evening."

"Are long coats in fashion suddenly?" Courtney stared after the woman.

"I certainly hope not," Jenna said.

"For more reasons than one." Mr. Finch started to lead the sisters up the road.

"What do you mean?" Angie asked the man.

To help steady himself, Mr. Finch slid his arm through Angie's. "Well, for one, it will make our investigation more difficult if everyone in town starts going around in long coats."

"And what's another reason?" Angie questioned.

Finch responded with a twinkle in his eye. "The style of the garment is hideous."

The comment set off a round of squeals and guffaws from the four sisters as they made their way up the small hill to the van.

***

ELLIE HAD prepared a pan of meat lasagna and a lentil and vegetable pie. The mouth-watering smell of the dinner baking in the oven filled the air. Mr. Finch sat at the table with a hot cup of tea and the two cats sat on top of the refrigerator. Angie was mixing dough in a large metal bowl.

"What kind of cookies are you making?" Courtney was washing lettuce in the sink for the salad.

"Nut." Angie stirred the dough with a wooden spoon. "In honor of the nuts who have recently come to town."

Courtney laughed as she dried the lettuce on the counter.

Tom and Jenna were sitting at the kitchen island leaning over Jenna's laptop. "Guess what?" she asked the group. "There isn't anything on the internet about a Walter Withers except for one thing. It says he was born in the UK and moved to Australia. He was a landscape artist. He died in 1914."

"I don't think that's our man," Courtney joked.

"Is that all the info out there?" Angie asked.

"For the most part." Tom looked at the entries on the screen. "These other things aren't about the man staying here at the B and B."

"I wonder." Mr. Finch stroked Circe's black fur. She had jumped off the fridge and curled up in the man's lap.

Everyone turned to Finch.

"I wonder if Mr. Withers is playing a joke on us. Perhaps he takes on a new name wherever he goes."

"I saw his ID though. It said Walter Withers on it." Ellie opened the oven door and slid out the lasagna and the lentil pie.

"His address must be on the ID. Did you notice it?" Jenna swiveled her stool around to face her sister. "Doesn't he have to list his address on the B and B guest card he fills in?"

Ellie frowned. "He told me he was in between apartments since he had to travel so extensively. I didn't need a zip code to verify his credit card because he paid in cash. In full, for the month."

"He's clever," Angie sighed. "Look up Clarence and Angelina Crosswort. See if you can find anything on the internet about them. I can't believe they rented the house right next to the one that burned down last night. It's a strange coincidence."

"And you thought you saw them in the second floor window." Courtney tossed the salad ingredients. "Why wouldn't they come out of the house last night to see what was happening?"

"Maybe it was my imagination. Maybe no one was in the house at all." Angie added the dry ingredients to the bowl and mixed them. "I felt bad for scaring Gloria when I rushed up on her in the dark."

Courtney looked at Angie. "How well do you know Gloria?"

Angie was aghast. "It's not her. She's not involved in the fires."

"How can you be sure?" Courtney cocked her

head.

Before Angie could reply, Jenna tapped some more at her laptop keyboard. Tom leaned over her shoulder and then straightened. "Nothing at all on the internet about the Crossworts."

Ellie's voice was high-pitched. "How can there be nothing? There isn't one thing?"

"Come look if you like. Nothing comes up." Tom faced Angie. "Are you sure you got their names right?"

"I'm sure." Angie rolled the cookie dough into small balls and placed them on the baking sheet. "It's exactly as I suspected it would be. Nothing to go on."

"These aren't normal people." Tom put his hand on Jenna's shoulder. "Stay away from them."

"We can't." Courtney carried the salad bowl to the kitchen island. "One is living in our house and the other two keep showing up in Angie's bake shop."

Ellie groaned and plopped into the chair opposite Mr. Finch. She put her head in her hands. "What are we going to do?"

"Well, these people haven't done anything wrong." Finch put his teacup on its saucer.

Courtney took salad dressing out of the refrigerator. "Except lie about their names and where they came from."

"But that isn't a crime," Finch said. "I don't think so anyway. These people may very well be harmless. However, in case they *aren't* harmless, we will keep our eyes on them and remain suspicious."

Euclid arched his back and let out a hiss.

"That isn't comforting," Ellie told the orange cat. She looked off across the room. "Do the police always have to bring us unwanted news?"

Angie gave Ellie a wary look. "Why are you mentioning the police?"

The back doorbell rang and Courtney went to see who it was. She returned with Officer Talbot.

Angie raised an eyebrow at Ellie. The tall blonde had recently started making statements out of the blue and then moments later, what she mentioned happened or appeared.

"Evening." The officer removed his hat. "Chief Martin asked me to come over." He cleared his throat. "One of us will be stationed out front of the Victorian each night for a while. We'll be sitting in a squad car most of the time, but we'll be strolling around the grounds now and then throughout the night. Chief Martin thought it best, for the time being, due to recent circumstances going on in town. He thought your guests may be concerned about the recent fires and would feel more at ease if there was a police presence out front. He'd like to stop by tomorrow and talk to you."

Angie thanked the officer and saw him out. When she returned, she looked at her family. "Well."

"That isn't comforting either." Ellie moaned.

"It is comforting." Courtney took salt and pepper from the cabinet. "Chief Martin takes care of us." She smiled. "Although, we do pretty well taking care of ourselves."

"I'm not sure how reassuring the police car out front will be." Tom held Jenna's hand in his. "It might make the guests worry that they're in real danger."

Angie's shoulders drooped. "I think the chief is using the guests' concern as a cover for him really being worried about us."

"I'm worried about our house." Jenna looked at Tom. "It's always empty. It could be a target if someone is actually setting fires around town."

Tom said, "I thought the same thing. I'll bring more lamps and floor lights over there tomorrow morning and we can keep them lit all night. I'll also install some security lighting around the perimeter of the house. We'll keep those on all night as well."

Jenna nodded. "Good idea."

Courtney put the salad and salad plates on a tray and headed for the hallway, but paused at the table where Ellie was sitting. "You might want to start practicing your telekinesis. If anyone comes at us with a weapon, it might come in handy if your skills are in good shape."

Ellie let out a long groan. "We need a plan, one that doesn't involve me."

CHAPTER 12

Angie could feel the Crossworts approaching the bake shop before they even opened the door and walked in. When the bell jingled, Angie looked at the entrance out of the corner of her eye. Dread ran through her body and she let out a sigh. Louisa started over to the old couple's table, but Angie placed her hand on the young woman's arm to stop her.

"I'll take care of them today." Angie pushed her shoulders back and plastered a smile on her face. She advanced across the room as if she was going into battle. "Good morning." She set down two white mugs on the table. "I'm Angie Roseland. I've been meaning to introduce myself."

The couple seemed to shrink down in their seats, their eyes wide. The gray-haired man wore his usual huge, dark overcoat. The woman's brown winter coat looked threadbare. Her eyes were sunken in her face and her skin had an almost yellow tinge to its appearance. Dark circles showed beneath the lower lids. Angie wondered if the woman was ill.

"Coffee?" Angie held a coffee pot in her right hand and waited for one of them to respond.

The woman turned away and looked out the window. The man gave a curt nod of his head and Angie filled the two mugs. "You're new to town?"

Again, the man gave the slightest of nods. Nervous energy poured off of him and it felt to Angie like a wall of dark fog was enveloping her. She took a tiny step back.

"Where are you living?" She asked even though she knew very well where the couple had rented a home.

The man raised his skinny arm and gestured. "Edge of town," he croaked.

Angie nodded. She thought that was an odd way of describing the area where their new house was located since it wasn't that far from the center of Sweet Cove. Angie pressed on. "There was a fire last night. Did you see it?"

The man shook his head. The woman was still gazing out of the window.

"Angie," Louisa called to her from behind the counter. She held up a twenty dollar bill. "Change?"

Angie nodded and before she headed to the back room to get more change from the safe she said, "I didn't get your names."

The man hunched over the tabletop whispering to the woman across from him and he pretended

97

not to hear. Angie waited for several seconds and then gave up.

"Have you been able to get anything out of them?" Angie asked Louisa.

"Nothing really. They requested coffee the first day they came in. Every morning when they show up I just fill their mugs and say some pleasantries. Now that I think of it, they never say a word to me." Louisa moved down the counter to wait on a customer. "Takes all kinds, I guess."

The morning passed in a flash of busyness and just before noon, Chief Martin showed up. He made eye contact with Angie and took the table at the far end of the room. Customers asked him questions about the fires in town and he answered calmly and reassuringly. Angie carried over a mug of tea and a chicken salad sandwich with a cup of tomato bisque and sat down across from him. "Thanks for the police car in front of the house at night."

The chief sipped from his mug. "I know you probably don't like it, but humor me."

Angie smiled and then asked, "Was the fire set last night?"

The chief let out a big sigh. "It doesn't seem so. The fire must have been smoldering for some time and once it kicked in, it took off. By the time the firefighters got through the front door, the smoke was already down to the floor, banked all the way down. The fire chief said it was unusual that the fire spread so fast before the call came in from a neighbor. He thinks it started on the first floor."

"A cigarette maybe?"

"Possibly."

"No gasoline or some type of accelerant?" Angie kept her voice low so the other customers couldn't hear.

Chief Martin shook his head. "None at the town common fire either."

"I wonder what we smelled when we were there?" Angie pondered.

"It's pretty unusual that both of these fires took off so fast. It's surprising behavior for fire to flare so rapidly without an accelerant." The chief's eyes looked tired and worry etched itself in lines across his forehead. "The fire chief finds it odd, too. He wonders what took so long for someone to notice the fire on Greenhill Road. The whole thing doesn't seem right."

"I told you about that odd couple who comes in here every morning?" Angie leaned in. "They told Betty Hayes that their names are Clarence and Angelina Crosswort, but when we looked them up on the internet, nothing comes up about them. Nothing." She told the chief that the couple gave Betty a false address for their former residence. "Guess the address of the house they just rented in Sweet Cove." Angie paused for effect. "The house to the right of the home that burned down last night."

The chief's jaw dropped. He put his sandwich back on the plate and wiped his fingers on his napkin. "We'll run them through the database."

"Don't be surprised if nothing comes up." Angie looked defeated. "You know, I thought I saw someone in the Crosswort house last night in the second floor window. It might have been my imagination though."

"But you don't think so."

Angie shrugged one shoulder.

"My officers went to the neighboring houses last night to ask people to step out in case the fire spread. I went to that house myself and rang the bell. No one answered the door."

"I guess they didn't want to come outside." Angie's mouth turned down.

The two discussed the person in the dark coat who frightened Ellie the night of the scarecrow fire and Angie reported that Gloria from the hair salon was wearing a long woolen poncho last night. "She can't be involved, but I wanted you to be aware that there's more than one person wearing a long dark coat around here."

Angie went on to tell the chief about the odd B and B guest, Walter Withers, and how his name seemed fake and that he had no address. "He paid cash for the guest room so Ellie doesn't have any credit card info on the man."

The chief reached into his pocket and took out a small pad. He removed a pen from his jacket pocket and wrote the names Angie had shared with him on the paper. "I suppose there isn't anything on the internet on Withers either?" He picked up his soup spoon and started in on the tomato bisque.

"Only if he's a painter who died in 1914."

The chief kept his head bent over his soup cup, but lifted his eyes to Angie and rolled them. "We asked the businesses around the common for their security tapes. Some looked like they might be helpful because the cameras had a view of the corner of the common."

"But they weren't?"

Chief Martin let out a sigh. "We watched the tapes. Right around the time the scarecrows would have been set up and lit on fire, there seems to have been an electrical glitch."

Angie made a face.

"Almost like the power that fed the security cameras went out."

"Could the tapes have been tampered with?"

"Three different businesses gave us their tapes. The same thing occurred on all three. They're all blank during the time period in question."

"Blank?" Angie couldn't believe it.

"Snowy is a better description." The chief rubbed his temple.

A chill skittered over Angie's skin and she ran her hands over her arms to warm them. "How can that be? All three tapes?"

"We have a technician looking into it."

"There's not much to go on, is there?"

"That hasn't stopped us before."

"That brings up something else." Angie glanced around the shop to be sure no one was eavesdropping. "Mr. Finch worries that the troublemaker might be someone from the past." She held the chief's eyes. "Nana's past."

Chief Martin straightened.

"Is there any case that Nana worked on where someone might want to take revenge on us? Now that we're living in Sweet Cove? Now that we're helping you with cases?" Angie bit her lower lip. "Maybe someone doesn't like it."

The chief sat quietly for almost a full minute. "Mr. Finch could be on to something. I'll go through the old paperwork. See if anything stands out."

"There's something else."

Chief Martin's eyebrows shot up.

"Circe found a sprig of mistletoe at the common fire."

"Mistletoe?" The chief shook his head, confused.

"And we noticed that mistletoe is growing in one of the trees in our back garden."

The chief looked completely blank not understanding where Angie was going with this. He tilted his head in question.

Angie asked, "Is it okay if I go walk around the burned house on Greenhill Road? Look for mistletoe?"

"What is its significance? Why would it be at the locations of the fires?"

Angie leveled her eyes at the chief. "It has magical qualities."

Anyone else would have chuckled at Angie's statement, but the chief was aware that not everything in the universe was understandable and that some things moved through the world that were hidden from most people. "I'll make a call. There's an officer on duty at the burned house and the fire investigators are almost done there. Maybe wait a day or so or the investigators won't give you access. Of course, you aren't allowed inside the house. Contain yourself to the outside."

"Okay. I might bring the others. And the cats."

The chief nodded. "I'd prefer if you didn't go there alone and please don't go there in the dark." The chief's lips were tight. "Any other tidbits to share?"

Angie shook her head. "That's it. For now."

Chief Martin sucked in a long breath. "We'll figure it out."

Angie gave the chief a little smile. "We always do."

She wished she felt as hopeful as she sounded.

CHAPTER 13

The late afternoon light filtered through the branches of the trees and long shadows began to form across the lawn. Ellie, Jenna, and Angie stood in the rear garden beneath the tall, old oak tree.

"Right there." Angie pointed. "See on the upper branches. The greenery with the little white berries."

Ellie squinted. Her hand shaded her eyes from the low rays hitting her in the face. "That stuff? I've never noticed that up there before." She put her other hand on her hip in an indignant pose.

"Well, the leaves were out on the trees in spring and summer. Most of them have fallen off, so the mistletoe is more visible now." Jenna followed her sisters' gaze up into the high branches.

"If it was there before, I would have seen it," Ellie grumped. "I've been working out here in this garden for months."

"It didn't just spring up overnight." As soon as the words were out of her mouth, Angie wondered if it actually did just appear one night. She eyed the green plant on the tree suspiciously.

"It looks mature. There's a good amount of it up there." Jenna's skepticism could be heard in her tone. "It had to be growing there for a while."

"It's parasitic?" Ellie made a face like she'd eaten something bad.

"That's what Rufus told us," Angie said.

"Are you sure it's mistletoe?" Ellie wasn't convinced, "I didn't know it grew in this part of the country."

"That's why we called the arborist." Jenna turned when she heard the sound of a car engine in their driveway. "Here's the guy now."

A white truck parked in front of the carriage house and a trim, middle-aged man stepped out. "Afternoon." He walked over to where the girls were standing.

Before the man could introduce himself, Ellie pointed. "It's up in this tree. Is that mistletoe? How long has it been up there?"

The man tried to stifle a grin. "I'm Ted, the arborist." He shook hands with the three sisters. "I'll go up and have a look." He went to the back of his truck and removed some equipment. Before they knew it, the man was high in the tree.

"It's mistletoe alright." The man called down to the girls. "What do you want to do about it? You want it removed?"

Ellie and Angie spoke at the same time.

"Yes," Ellie told the arborist.

"Leave it there," Angie replied.

The girls looked at each other.

"What's the harm in having it in the tree?" Jenna asked.

"It will kill the oak." Ellie turned her face upwards to the man in the tree. "Will it kill the oak?"

"Not necessarily." The man fiddled with the plant. "Just keep an eye on the tree. If it seems distressed I can come back."

"How long has it been there?" Ellie asked.

"It's mature. It had to be here for a while." The man started down the tree to the ground.

Angie and Jenna gave Ellie the eye.

"I don't believe it," Ellie was adamant. "I know I would have seen it there before this."

"Then how did it suddenly get there? He says it mature." Jenna shoved her hands into her jacket pockets.

"It *is* mature." The man looked from one sister to the other. "You sure you don't want it removed? If it bothers you, it wouldn't take me long to do it."

"What's going on?" a man's voice spoke.

The girls and the arborist turned to see Walter Withers walking up to them.

"We wanted to know if that plant in the tree is mistletoe." Ellie's eyes were dark.

"I could have saved you the money." Withers glanced up into the oak's branches. "It's mistletoe. You aren't going to cut it out, are you?"

As Angie turned to walk the arborist to the truck, she asked Withers, "Why shouldn't we cut it out?" She wondered why Withers seemed alarmed that the mistletoe might be removed.

"Because." Withers' eyes bored into Angie's. "It's magic."

"Magic, Mr. Withers?" Ellie pursed her lips and shook her head. "Well, if you want some of it to cast any spells, you can rest assured. For now, we're leaving it in the tree."

"Wise decision. You never know when you might need it." Withers headed down the driveway. "I'll be out this evening."

The sisters watched him go.

"What on earth?" Ellie walked over to the fire pit and sank into one of the Adirondack chairs. "Is he trying to get a rise out of us or is he crazy?"

Jenna sat down next to her sister. "Or can he really do spells?"

Angie picked up a piece of mistletoe that had gotten stuck in the arborist's boot. "If Withers could do spells, I don't think he'd broadcast the fact." She looked the plant over and then lay it down on one of the fire pit stones. "Why are we having so much trouble picking up on things? I feel like my sensations are blocked."

"Things definitely seem confused." Jenna leaned back in the chair. "Mixed up ... messed up."

"I've felt out of sorts for days." Ellie spotted Mr. Finch approaching through the trees along the walkway that he'd had put in between his Willow Street house and the Victorian. Circe padded along beside the man. "Here comes Mr. Finch. Maybe he can help us figure out what's wrong."

Finch joined the girls around the fire pit. Circe sat in his lap and purred. The girls explained their feelings of being blocked and unable to sense things about the current case.

"It feels like the time when the bomb was in the house next to yours." Angie pushed her hair back from her face. "Remember how we couldn't make sense of anything?"

Finch nodded. "That case involved many people with sad backgrounds. The negative energy from our past cases has acted like static and made us unable to read the things that float on the air. Perhaps such things are blocking our abilities again."

"We need to clear it out." Courtney walked into the backyard from the rear door of the house with Euclid following behind her. "How should we do it? Last time, we made Angie bake us something. It was something sweet and light, remember? It helped us rise above the negativity and cleared our heads."

Euclid jumped up on the fire pit stones and sat, listening to the conversation.

"Hmm." Finch tapped his index finger against his chin. "Miss Angie, would you like to try and work your magic, again?"

Angie smiled. "Just don't let Mr. Withers hear the word magic." She stood up. "What should I make this time?"

"It's fall. Halloween time," Jenna observed. "I think it should be something appropriate to the season."

"Something with pumpkin?" Courtney suggested.

Finch cocked his head. "Should it have a bit of spice or fire to it, since we're dealing with fires in this case?"

Euclid and Circe trilled their approval.

"I have an idea." Angie grinned and led the entourage into the kitchen where baking magic was about to take place.

***

ANGIE BUSTLED in the cabinets pulling out a glass bowl, wooden spoons, and different ingredients while Jenna, Ellie, and Finch sat at the kitchen island watching. The two cats jumped up on the fridge to keep an eye on the proceedings.

"What's cookin, Sis?" Courtney stood next to her sister trying to figure out what she was about to bake.

Angie pushed an apron over her head. "Chocolate pumpkin bread with spicy Aztec chocolate."

"Genius. I love it." Courtney rubbed her hands

together in anticipation. "What can I get for you?"

Angie listed the other ingredients she needed and her youngest sister went to retrieve them. She carried the things back to the island and piled them next to the flour and sugar. "Remember to put intention into your baking, Sis. We need to clear away the heaviness and static so we can sense what's going on in town."

Mr. Finch made tea for everyone while Angie measured and mixed.

"I found a box of Mom's stuff in the carriage house storage room the other day." Ellie yawned. The girls' mother had passed away several years ago in an accident in Boston. When Angie inherited the Victorian from one of her regular customers who turned out to be a relative of theirs, her sisters had moved up to Sweet Cove to join her and lots of unpacked boxes were still stored away.

"There's room to move around in there now that the bake shop things have been moved out and put in place in the new store." Angie poured some vanilla into a measuring spoon. When she'd lost the lease on her old café, she'd had to store her equipment in the carriage house until the renovations were completed to house her bakery in part of the Victorian.

Ellie said, "There are some of Mom's clothes in the box, some of her scarves. There's also a box with some of her jewelry. I looked through it."

Jenna perked up. "Jewelry? I'd like to see that."

"The box is in the sunroom. When Angie finishes, let's all go take a look." Ellie added some milk to her tea. "We can each pick the things we'd like to keep."

When the bread went into the oven, they all filed into the sunroom and Ellie placed the box on the coffee table for her sisters so they could look through the items.

"Are there things you want?" Courtney asked Ellie.

"There's a necklace I'd like if no one else is interested in it." Ellie reached into the box and retrieved a smooth wooden jewelry case. She opened it and tipped the pieces of jewelry onto the table. "There's nothing valuable, mostly just costume jewelry. They're pretty things though."

"Mom was always stylish." Jenna fondly recalled how put-together their mother always looked.

Ellie lifted a small white leather box from the table. "Here's the piece I like." She opened the box and held up a simple silver chain with an oval cabochon containing a pearly white stone. "I don't remember Mom ever wearing this, but I know she had it on when she died."

"What's the stone?" Angie peered at it. "It looks like an opal."

"I don't know what it is. I don't think it's an opal though." Ellie held it up to her neck.

Jenna eyed the stone. "I don't know what it is either. Maybe moonstone?"

111

"It's lovely, Miss Ellie." Finch smiled. "It fits you."

"I think you should have it," Jenna said. "You're the one who looks most like Mom. It looks at home on you."

Angie and Courtney agreed and Ellie undid the clasp and put the necklace around her neck. Her finger tips ran over the smooth stone. The sisters could see a few tears glistening at the corners of Ellie's eyes.

"Mom would want you to have it." Angie hugged her sister. "Look how the stone shimmers in the light. It's so pretty."

The girls inspected the rest of the things in the box until the oven timer went off indicating that the bread was finished baking. Everyone traipsed into the kitchen, and when the bread was cool, Angie sliced it and placed the pieces on plates.

"Shall we take the treats outside?" Mr. Finch asked. "It might be helpful if we sit under the moon, eat our bread, and connect with the natural world."

The cats led the way to the chairs around the fire pit. The sisters and Finch sat and enjoyed the baked goodies. Even the cats ate small slices of bread from white porcelain saucers. Ellie had brought blankets out for each person to wrap up in to keep warm in the cool night air. Angie was praised for her efforts and the bread disappeared quickly from the plates. The group sat quietly in the moonlight listening to the rustle of leaves in the breeze and the hoots of an owl. They could even hear the ebb and flow of ocean waves on the sand several blocks away down Beach Street.

"We should do this more often," Courtney observed. "It's so peaceful."

Euclid and Circe trilled.

Angie could feel the powerful bonds between her, her sisters, Mr. Finch, and the two cats and wondered how it was possible for anything to ever be wrong in their world.

They were about to find out just how wrong things could be.

CHAPTER 14

Angie woke with a start, the frightening dream slowly fading out of her mind like the starlight that filtered through the glass of her bedroom window, soft and intangible. She couldn't recall the details of the nightmare, only the vague feelings of alarm and fear that startled her awake.

Angie sat up and stretched taking a look at the clock next to her bed. She felt wired and alert and knew it would take her a long time to fall back to sleep only to be jolted awake in two hours by the alarm. She steeled herself to the inevitable feeling of drowsiness that she knew would come over her in the early afternoon.

Angie pushed back the covers and got out of bed padding to the dresser where she'd left the murder mystery book she'd been reading. She carried it to her bed and placed it on top of the blanket. She was about to crawl back under her quilt when a swirl of leaves blew past her window and she went to look out at the clear, chilly October night. Pushing the opaque curtain to the side, Angie glanced down at the Adirondack chairs set in the grass around the fire pit where the family had enjoyed the bread she'd made last night. The anxious feelings from her dream had disappeared. Gazing at the back garden, the lovely view filled her with a sense of calm and ease.

The moonlight shimmered off of something that was on top of the fire pit stones and it caught Angie's eye. It was the sprig of mistletoe she'd placed there hours ago. The white berries glistened. Mesmerized by the shining berries, she watched as they grew brighter and brighter and Angie was sure she saw the shadow of Ellie's face reflected in them. After a few moments, the blazing white light became almost painful to look at and forced her to shut her eyes.

Angie woke to the sound of the bleating alarm clock. She reached over to turn it off and after a few minutes, she flicked on the bedside light and dragged herself out of bed. She grabbed her robe and shuffled to the door heading for the shower. Angie noticed the mystery book lying on top of her dresser and she stopped and stared at it. Shifting her eyes, she looked over to the bed and then back to the dresser. *Funny, I'm sure I brought the book over to the bed last night.* She yawned and shrugged and stepped out into the hall, dragging herself to the shower.

***

ANGIE HAD already started the first batch of muffins when Ellie came into the kitchen. "Morning." Ellie stifled a yawn and reached for a big glass bowl. She carried strawberries, blueberries, grapes, and honeydew melon to the counter and started to slice the melon to prepare the fruit salad. The cats sat at attention on the fridge watching the girls work.

Angie greeted her sister and started adding ingredients to her stainless steel bowl for a new batch of muffins just as Courtney stumbled into the kitchen, her hair dripping from the shower. Reaching for a cereal bowl she carried it the counter where she filled it with her favorite cereal, sliced some banana over it, and added milk. She sank into a chair and spooned her breakfast into her mouth.

"Good morning to you, too," Ellie said.

Courtney waved to her. "I'm still asleep," she managed to say in between mouthfuls. She pushed her wet hair back from her forehead. "I had the weirdest dream last night."

"Were you flying in your dream again?" Angie smiled.

"No, that hasn't happened for a while." Courtney brushed a bit of milk from her lip with the back of her hand. "It was different than any dream I can remember. I was standing at the window of my bedroom looking down into the backyard."

Angie's head snapped up and she stared at

Courtney.

"The leaves were swirling around. There was a piece of mistletoe on the fire pit stones. Its white berries started to shine, really bright."

The cats trilled.

Ellie stopped slicing and turned to her sister, a serious, wide-eyed look on her face. She held a strawberry in one hand and a small knife in the other.

Courtney lifted another spoonful of cereal to her mouth. "The mistletoe berries got brighter and brighter until I couldn't look at them anymore. The dream made me feel peaceful. Weird, huh?" Staring down at her bowl, she chewed and swallowed. "But the weirdest part was I could see Ellie in the white light of the berries." Courtney shook her head and chuckled. "I can't even escape my sisters in my dreams."

Neither sister spoke.

Courtney looked up and saw their expressions. "What?"

Angie and Ellie just stared.

"What's wrong with you two?" Courtney frowned.

Angie and Ellie exchanged glances.

"You had that dream, too?" Angie asked Ellie.

Ellie put her hand on her chest and gave the slightest of nods.

"Wait." Courtney sat up straight staring at Ellie. "You dreamed the same dream as me?" She shifted her eyes away from Ellie and looked at Angie. "Did you?"

"Maybe." Angie placed the wooden spoon on the counter.

Courtney's eyes went as wide as saucers. "You did." She almost shrieked with delight. "The three of us had the same dream. How cool is this." Courtney leaped from her chair. "I'm going to go wake up Jenna and ask if she dreamed it, too."

"Jenna will kill you," Angie warned, but it was too late. Courtney was already out the door of the kitchen and heading for the staircase.

Ellie said in a voice barely above a whisper, "What does it mean? Why is my face in the berries? Why did we dream the same dream?"

"I guess we managed to clear away the fog and static that was blocking our ability to pick up on things." Angie lifted the spoon and began to mix. "Now we just need to figure out how to translate it all."

"Do you have a recipe that can help us with that?" Ellie returned to slicing.

"Not that I know of," Angie said. "I think we'll have to rely on logic and reasoning."

Ellie placed the fruit salad in a serving bowl and gently mixed. "What does your logic and reasoning say about my face in the berries?"

"I have to give that some thought."

With a wide grin, Courtney poked her head into the kitchen. "Jenna wasn't too happy about me

118

waking her up. But guess what? She had the dream, too. I have to leave in a few minutes for the candy store to do the morning setup. We all need to talk tonight." She retreated to go and get ready for work.

"This case is so confusing." Ellie sighed. "There are hardly any suspects that you can talk to. How will you figure it out?"

"You mean, how will *we* figure it out?" Angie poured the muffin batter into the tins.

"No, I mean *you*."

The back door opened and in strolled Mr. Finch. "Good morning, girls." He looked up at the cats. "Good morning, my fine felines." Finch took a tea cup from the cabinet and put on a kettle of water. As he leaned against the counter, he hung his cane on the lip edge of the countertop. "I had the strangest dream last night."

Angie and Ellie shared a quick glance.

A shiver of unease ran down Angie's back. "Did you, Mr. Finch? Would you like to tell us about it?" She already knew what Finch would say about the dream.

"It was nighttime in the dream and I was staring down into the yard from my bedroom window when I noticed a sprig of mistletoe glowing bright white." Finch leaned against the counter as he recalled the image from his dream. "It became brighter and brighter until I could no longer look at it. I had to avert my eyes."

"Was that the whole dream?" Ellie asked.

Finch looked across the room at the tall blond and then he cocked his head. "Strange. I remember seeing the faint likeness of your face in the bright light." The tea kettle whistled and Finch removed it from the burner and poured steaming water into his China cup. "Isn't it funny that I would dream such a thing?" He added cream and a bit of sugar and stirred. When he lifted the cup to his lips, he noticed the girls were staring at him. He set the cup back on its saucer. "Oh. It means something?"

Angie said, "We all had exactly the same dream last night."

"All four of you?" Finch's bushy eyebrows rose up. "And has the meaning been determined?"

"We haven't gotten that far yet." Angie slid the muffin tin into the oven.

The cats jumped off the fridge and watched Finch fix his toast with butter and raspberry jam. Euclid and Circe each received a small dab of butter which they licked up with vigor. "I am not going into the candy store until after noon today. I believe I will pay a visit to the town library."

"Are you after a new book to read, Mr. Finch?" Ellie asked.

"I am going to do some research. On mistletoe." Mr. Finch ran his hand over Circe's dark fur. "Perhaps tonight we should have a family meeting?"

Angie lifted the large tray of muffins and headed to the bake shop. "It's time to put our heads together. We need to figure this out."

Before it's too late.

CHAPTER 15

The late afternoon sunlight streamed in the windows where Angie and Jenna sat at the desks in the jewelry room. Angie was paging through a book on Sweet Cove's history looking for information about the house that Jenna and Tom had purchased. Jenna was searching the internet for land records and house sale transactions.

"I'm coming up empty." Jenna groaned. "All there is on the land records is the sale from the town to Tom, and prior to that, a takeover notice passing the deed to the town of Sweet Cove for non-payment of taxes." She looked over at Angie. "Are you finding anything?"

"Well, there's a picture of your house in this book." Angie got up and put the open book on the table in front of her sister. "Look how nice it was back then."

A picture of Jenna and Tom's house was in the chapter on "Homes of Sweet Cove." The house stood in all its glory, freshly painted and carefully landscaped.

"If the house was still in this condition, we never could have afforded it." Jenna bent close to the picture to better see the details of the windows and woodwork. "I wish the photograph it was in color. I'd love to see what the original shades of the house were."

"It's going to be gorgeous when you and Tom finish the renovation."

Jenna let out a sigh. "I'm worried about how long that's going to take and how much money it's going to cost us." She pulled her long brown hair over her shoulder and started to braid it. "I hope we haven't bitten off more than we can chew."

"You two can move into the carriage house if you want." An impish grin formed on Angie's face. "You can live there for how many hundreds of years it will take you to complete the house." She scooted a few feet away to avoid Jenna's attempt to swat her. Still standing out of her sister's reach, Angie asked, "Did you read the little caption in the book under the house picture?"

Jenna looked back to the historical book and scanned the short paragraph under the photograph. She read aloud. *The lovely Queen Anne on Beach Street is a twelve room beautifully designed home with a large veranda and a three-story octagonal tower. Built in 1897, it is finely finished, landscaped, and maintained.* Jenna frowned. "Not a word about the owners. Maybe we can find out more at the town hall."

Angie leaned back against the desk. "The Crossworts didn't come into the bake shop this morning."

"It's the first morning they've missed since moving to town?"

Angie nodded. "It worries me. At least when they come in, I know where they are. Why didn't they show up today? What are they up to?"

"The woman looks kind of sickly." Jenna moved the historical book to the corner of her desk and closed down her laptop. "Maybe she wasn't up to coming to the bake shop today."

"Maybe." Angie reached for her jacket on the back of the chair. "Before we go to the town hall, I think we should make a detour, well, two detours."

Jenna looked questioningly at her sister.

"We haven't been to Robin's Point in a while. I think it would help us. I need to feel the thrumming in my blood." Lines of worry creased the corners of Angie's eyelids. "I'm worried, Jenna. Somebody wants to hurt us. I can feel it getting closer. We need to stop it."

Jenna's heart pounded. She stood up with a determined look. "Don't worry, I'm right beside you. We'll figure it out." She reached for her car keys. "Let's get started."

***

JENNA'S OLD junk of a car seemed to rattle as

they drove up Beach Street to the main street of Sweet Cove. "You said two detours. Where else do you want to go?"

"Greenhill Road."

"Now?" Jenna stopped at the intersection.

"Chief Martin said the fire inspection is done. We can walk around the outside of the house without anyone questioning us about why we're there." Angie looked out the passenger side window at the quaint brick walkways, stores and restaurants of the pretty town. "I'd also like to spy on the Crosswort house."

"Where do you want to go first?" While waiting for Angie's instructions, Jenna looked in the rearview mirror to be sure there wasn't a car behind them.

"Robin's Point."

Jenna turned left and headed down to the Sweet Cove Resort where they parked and walked over to the point. A cold wind blew off the ocean whipping the girls' hair around their heads. They stood at the edge of the sandy cliff and watched the waves crash against the beach below.

"Want to jump in?" Jenna kidded.

Angie eyed her. "After you."

Jenna grabbed her sister's arm and pretended to push her off the cliff. Angie mock-fought her and the two fell backward onto the grass laughing. They stared at the darkening blue autumn sky and rested quietly on their backs for a few minutes.

"Do you feel it?" Jenna asked. When on Robin's Point, Angie and Courtney could feel a humming or thrumming running through their veins. It was like a distant drum beating out a rhythm. Their Nana once owned a small cottage on the point and, being on the spot where it used to stand, made the girls feel close to her.

"Yeah." Angie's eyes were closed and her breathing was slow and rhythmic, matching the beat of the thrumming. Sometimes the feeling acted as an early warning system alerting Angie and Courtney to be on guard in a situation or to be wary of a particular person.

After fifteen minutes, the cold ground became uncomfortable and Jenna sat up. "Are you ready to go?" she asked gently.

Angie's eyes opened and she pushed herself up. "I'm ready. Let's go inspect the houses on Greenhill Road."

Jenna pulled on her sister's hand helping her to her feet. They walked arm in arm to the car and in ten minutes, they parked in front of the burned and ruined house. Angie gazed at the sad structure, its paint bubbled and peeling, the shutters askew, and windows broken. Dark burnt sections obliterated the color of the paint on different sections of the house. The lawn was rutted and ripped up where the fire trucks had stood. The darkening sky added to the gloomy atmosphere.

The girls got out and stood staring at the

building.

Jenna said, "If you wanted a creepy Halloween backdrop, this is it."

They walked around the far side of the house, careful not to trip in the ruts. Orange police tape was wound around the porch railings to warn against climbing the steps.

"What are we looking for?" Jenna glanced up at the second floor windows.

"Who knows?" Angie kicked at a lump of dirt as they made their way around the back of the house and along the other side. "That's the Crosswort place." The house stood in darkness. "I wonder if they've moved in yet. I'd love to look in the windows."

"You can go look." Jenna took a step back. "I'll watch you from here."

"I think I'm close enough." Angie led the way back to the front. "Do you pick up on anything?"

"Only that I'm cold and sort of creeped out." Jenna took a look at her watch. "The town hall will be closing soon. We'll have to go there tomorrow."

Angie let out a breath. "Let's go home."

The girls started for the car when Angie stopped short and whirled around to face the porch. "Look." She hurried to the steps.

Jenna followed. "Don't go on the porch."

Angie gingerly put a foot on the first step and put some weight on it. She did the same on the other treads and slowly moved across the porch to the front door.

"Angie." Jenna watched as her sister reached for the doorknob, lifted something off of it, and turned around. Angie raised her hand.

"What is it?" Jenna squinted trying to see in the dark. "What did you find?"

Angie shuffled carefully back to the steps and handed something to her.

Jenna took it in her hand. "Mistletoe? I thought Rufus said that mistletoe could protect against fires. I guess it didn't work."

"Take a good look at it." Angie came down off the porch. "I don't think it was here during the fire."

"Someone put it here afterwards? Why?"

Angie took a look around the lawn, at the Crossworts' front yard, and across the street. Her eyes darkened. "I bet it was put there for us to find." She raised an eyebrow. "The plot thickens." Angie led the way to Jenna's car.

Jenna did a three-point turn and started back up Greenhill Road. "Why would someone want us to find it? What does it mean?"

Angie watched out the window as the car sped past houses and trees when she suddenly sat up and swiveled to look back to where they'd come. "Keep going for another block and pull over."

"What? Why?" Jenna coasted to the side of the road and parked. "What do you see?"

"Two people are talking back there." Angie

opened the passenger side door and stepped out.

Jenna joined her on the sidewalk.

"One of them is wearing a long dark coat." Angie headed down the hill. "Stay close to the shadows. Go slow."

The girls moved quietly and stealthily until Angie lifted her hand to indicate they should stop. She whispered, "Let's go behind the trees over there."

The girls stepped into a grove of trees that shielded them from the view of the two people talking. They couldn't hear what was being said. Angie leaned down and peered between the branches. Anxiety gripped every muscle in her body.

She sucked in a breath and reached for her sister's arm. "It's Gloria."

"Who?"

"Gloria, our hair stylist. She was here the other night. She's talking to Walter Withers, our B and B guest." Angie turned to Jenna, her voice shaking. "What on earth are they doing together, on this street?"

CHAPTER 16

"Should we approach them?" Angie wondered how they would react if she and Jenna walked up.

Jenna peeked through the branches. "I don't know." She kept her voice low. "We probably shouldn't. They might be dangerous."

The girls tried to make out what the two people were saying to each other, but they were speaking too softly to pick up any of the words.

"Look. They're moving down the street." Angie craned her neck to watch. "We need to follow."

Jenna glanced back at her car. "I wish I brought the tire iron."

Angie tugged on her sister's sleeve and they crept along the street stepping into shadow and sidling up behind trees and bushes to maintain their cover. Gloria and Withers looked over their shoulders and then edged into the side yard of the Crossworts' house.

Hiding in the bushes across the street, the girls watched.

"What are they doing?" Jenna tried to keep them

in her sight.

"That's a very good question." Angie knelt on the lawn. "Withers is just visiting town. How do those two know each other?"

"A better question is why are they skulking around the Crossworts' yard?"

Angie slipped her phone out her pocket. "I'm going to text Chief Martin and tell him what's going on."

Less than a minute passed, when a reply came in from the chief. "Sit tight. I'm coming. Unmarked car."

Gloria and Withers disappeared around the back of the house and the girls lost sight of them. Angie lowered a branch. "I can't see where they went. Should we move closer?"

"Chief Martin said to sit tight." Jenna knelt beside her sister.

A car came down the road and the sisters heard the mechanical sound of a garage door rising. The car turned into the driveway of the property where the girls were hiding.

"We need to move." Jenna moved to a crouch position and shuffled out of the yard. "We can't get caught lurking here. People will think we set that fire."

Angie groaned and followed. When they reached the sidewalk, Chief Martin drove slowly down the street, and from inside the car, he gestured to the burned out house ahead. He pulled to the curb in front of the destroyed home and got out. Jenna and Angie hugged the shadows as they hurried to meet him.

"Gloria and Withers walked into the yard on the right side of the Crosswort place." Angie pointed. "They went to the back of the house and we lost sight."

"Stay here in front and keep an eye out. I'm going to walk around like I'm doing a routine check on this place." He nodded to the burned home. "Watch for them. See if they leave the Crosswort place when they notice me walking around here."

The chief flicked on his large black flashlight and started to circle the devastated home. The girls could occasionally hear a twig snap as the chief moved about making his rounds. In five minutes, he was back in front.

"Anything? Any movement?" Chief Martin asked.

The girls shook their heads.

"I didn't see any sign of them. They must have seen me and gone into the yard of the house behind the Crosswort.' Any doubt about their identities?"

Angie sighed. "I'm sure it was Gloria Harding and Walter Withers."

"Gloria's been living in town for years, her whole life, I think. Odd that she was here with Withers, but the reason could be harmless." The chief looked over at the Crosswort house which was shrouded in darkness. "Are those people ever home?"

"I can't believe Gloria could be a suspect in the fires." Angie frowned.

"Well, my years in law enforcement have taught me that sometimes people can surprise you, and not in good ways, but I've also learned not to jump to conclusions." The chief started for his vehicle. "Come on, I'll drop you at your car."

The chief decided to follow Jenna and Angie back to the Victorian so that they could have a chat with everyone to bring the group up to date. They drove the few minutes to Main Street and pulled into the B and B's driveway.

When the three reached the front porch, Ellie flung the door open. There was a cat standing on either side of her and the look on her face sent a chill down Angie's back.

"Now what?" Jenna asked.

Euclid and Circe let out low hisses.

When the girls and Chief Martin stepped into the foyer, they saw Tom standing in the dining room holding his phone.

"Tom's been trying to reach you." Ellie's face was pale. "Thank heavens you're okay."

Tom looked up, his face creased with worry. "I've been texting you."

Jenna rushed to his side. "Our phones have been on silent. What's wrong?"

Tom put his arm around her and let out a sigh. "Someone broke into our place."

Jenna's eyes filled with tears and her hand flew to her chest.

"There's no damage." Tom's lips turned up in a small smile as he tried to reassure his fiancé. "If there was, it wouldn't really matter anyway since the house is in such poor shape already." The big man rubbed Jenna's back. "Stuff's been moved around. Some of the old furniture upstairs has been tipped over, some drawers pulled out. That's all really." Tom pulled Jenna close. "I'm just glad you weren't in the house alone when the person broke in."

"Did you call it in?" Chief Martin was angry about the break-in and it showed on his face.

Tom nodded. "I told the officer to meet me here."

"Let's go sit in the family room where we can talk," Angie suggested. The family room was in the private part of the Victorian and she wanted to be out of earshot of any of the B and B guests, Walter Withers in particular, should any of them wander down to the living room.

Just as they all sat down, Courtney and Mr. Finch came in from their shift at the candy store and information was shared about the break-in at Jenna and Tom's house.

"I wonder if the break-in is related to the fires?" Courtney was in the easy chair with Euclid sitting on her lap. His orange plume twitched back and forth as he listened to the latest news.

"I would be inclined to say yes." Mr. Finch sat on one of the sofas next to Jenna and Tom. Circe sat on Jenna's lap, alert and attentive to the conversation. "Was anything stolen from your house?"

Tom looked at Jenna. "I didn't think of that. We don't keep anything there except tools and paint and such. Nothing seemed to be missing."

Jenna said, "We haven't gone through all of the dressers and bureaus that came with the house though, but I can't imagine anything valuable was left in the house."

The sisters made eye contact with one another wondering if there might be something else that someone might be looking for besides valuables.

Angie told the family about the visit to Greenhill Road. "Jenna and I went over to the burned-out house to look around. Guess what we found at the front door?"

Courtney's eyes narrowed. "Mistletoe."

Jenna gave her a surprised look. "Good guess."

"What else could it have been? That stuff is showing up everywhere."

Angie told them who they'd seen talking together on Greenhill Road.

"Gloria?" Ellie twisted the end of her hair. "She's involved?'

"I really can't believe it," Angie said. "I've never gotten any bad feelings from her. I just don't think she could be part of this mess." She took a look at the cats to see if they reacted to hearing the woman's name. They were both calm.

"How does she know Mr. Withers?" Ellie pulled her legs up under her. "Withers distinctly told me he didn't know anyone in Sweet Cove."

"He could have gone to the salon for a haircut and met her," Angie offered. "But why would they be on Greenhill Road together in the dark?"

Mr. Finch spoke. "I haven't run into Mr. Withers lately. Have you seen him much?"

Ellie straightened. "No. He's still a guest here, but I've barely seen him. He used to follow me around like a shadow, but now I barely run into him. He doesn't take breakfast in the mornings anymore and he seems to be gone most of the day."

Angie's face clouded. "I just remembered. I have a hair appointment with Gloria tomorrow. Maybe I'll cancel it."

"I think you should go." Chief Martin looked pensive. "There will be plenty of people around. She doesn't know that you suspect her. Have a chat. Maybe something will slip out."

"I'm going to go with you." Ellie pushed her hair over her shoulder. "I need a trim."

Angie made eye contact with Ellie and cocked her head. Ellie usually wanted to stay far away from trouble of any kind. "Why do you want to go?"

"I told you, I need a trim." Ellie made a face. "I don't really know why. I just know I'm going with you." She turned her hands up in a helpless gesture.

The cats trilled their approval.

Everyone stared at Ellie, but no one said a word. They weren't about to question someone's intuition, at least not the intuition of someone in this family.

CHAPTER 17

Angie opened the back door of the house to walk around the garden while she was waiting for Ellie to get ready to go to the hair salon. She spotted Professor Tyler standing near the fire pit looking up into the oak tree. He had a scowl on his face.

Angie watched him for a few moments before stepping out and saying hello.

The Professor startled momentarily. "Oh hello, Angie. It's a nice morning. I thought I'd get some air before heading off to the library."

"How is your research going?"

"Slow, but that's often the case." He gestured to the fire pit. "Do you use this often?"

"Pretty often. This weekend, we're planning to have drinks and desserts out here around the fire. Ellie likes to do that every weekend in October to celebrate the season. She'll let all the guests know which day and time."

"Very nice." The man seemed distracted. His eyes flicked about the yard and at the carriage house. "The yard is lovely."

"Ellie handles the landscaping and flowers. She does a nice job with the fall decorations."

"Mmm-hmm." The Professor nodded. "This is the first time I've been out here."

Euclid was inside near the back door. He howled to be let out. When Angie didn't respond, he let out a loud hiss.

"What's wrong with the cat?"

Angie was about to say that Euclid tended to get fussy when he didn't get his way, but she stopped herself as a little shiver ran along her spine. She eyed Professor Tyler and took Euclid's cue. "You haven't been out here before? Didn't I see you walking around in the garden just the other day?" Angie lied.

Professor Tyler blinked. He opened his mouth and then shut it. He gave Angie a smile. "Oh, right. I forgot." He shook his head. "I've been very distracted with my work lately."

Euclid howled again.

"Did you notice the mistletoe in the tree?" Angie used a conversational tone.

"What? You have mistletoe?" A cool breeze hit the two of them and the professor tucked the ends of his scarf inside his coat.

Angie pushed her hair out of her eyes and pointed up at the oak tree branches.

"Well, look at that." The professor took a few steps towards the driveway. "It's invasive you know. It will kill the oak tree if you don't get rid of

139

it. It happens quickly and then it's too late. You should have it removed." He strode away. "Must get to the library. See you later."

Angie watched him go wondering how so many people knew so much about mistletoe. She went inside the house through the back door. Euclid sat there, his eyes intent, his plume swishing across the floor, back and forth.

"Thanks for alerting me to the professor's lie." Angie nodded to the cat. "I'll keep my eye on him." Euclid, satisfied with her response, trilled, turned, and walked through the kitchen to the hall just as Ellie came into the room.

"I'm ready." Ellie lifted her jacket from the wall hook. "I thought I heard Euclid fussing down here."

"He doesn't like Professor Tyler."

Ellie stopped in the middle of zipping her jacket. "No?"

"Who knows why?" Angie shrugged. "But it won't hurt to be watchful when he's around."

***

"**KEEP ALERT**. See what you can pick up on when we go in. Watch Gloria. See if you notice anything suspicious." Angie eyed Ellie and she nodded as they opened the salon doors and stepped inside.

Angie was escorted to the chair in front of the

big wall mirror and as soon as she was seated, Gloria bustled over and covered the young woman with a dark blue cape. Gloria ran a comb though Angie's hair. "Gorgeous color. You are one lucky duck to have such natural, lovely hair tones."

The hair stylist was looking fashionably professional as usual. She had on black slacks, a pressed white blouse, and an unstructured black and white v-neck sweater. Her makeup was perfect and her hair nicely styled.

"Just a shaping?" Gloria reached for her scissors and chatted away with Angie.

Ellie sat two chairs down the aisle. She was making conversation with the stylist doing her hair, but she was listening intently to her sister's chat with Gloria.

"Any news on the fires?" Angie asked.

"Lots of speculation. No answers." Gloria snipped the ends off Angie's hair. "No arrests."

"The house is a total loss I hear."

"What a shame. It'll be knocked down. Such a waste."

"Do you know the new people who moved in recently next to the burned house?" Angie watched Gloria's face in the mirror.

"I didn't even know that house was a rental." Gloria lifted a lock of Angie's hair and cut a half inch off. "I wonder if the new neighbors are worried. Not the best way to be welcomed to a new neighborhood."

Angie agreed. "It's such a busy season in town, lots of people buzzing about. The B and B is full. We have a couple of interesting guests. A professor is staying with us. He's written books on the Salem Witch Trials."

"Such a fascinating topic."

"The other interesting guest is quite secretive about what he does for a living. Courtney is sure he works for the government in some secret job."

"He doesn't let on about his occupation?" Gloria seemed intrigued.

"No and he claims that he doesn't have a permanent address because he moves around all the time." Angie's eyes didn't leave the woman's face. "The name he gave us is actually the name of a long-dead painter."

Gloria's eyes widened. "Interesting. It must be coincidence that he has the same name."

"Or he's lying."

"Why would he lie?"

Angie said, "He might be a government spy or something."

Gloria chuckled. "Then he must be quite bored being in Sweet Cove unless he's investigating scarecrows being set on fire."

"That was a sight, wasn't it?" Angie tried to catch Gloria off guard.

"I'll say. It lit up the whole common." Gloria reached for a different pair of scissors.

Angie's throat tightened at the woman's answer.

142

Gloria had told Angie when they'd met at the house fire that she'd been in the next town on the night the five scarecrows were set up and she hadn't seen the fire on the common.

Angie asked a question before Gloria could realize her mistake. "Someone said they saw our secretive odd guest coming out of this salon. Do you know him? He says his name is Walter Withers."

Something fleeting flickered over the hair stylist's face and then she recovered. "Really? I don't recall anyone with that name."

Angie's heart sank. Until now, she'd never wanted to consider Gloria as a suspect. "Have you been back to look at the house that burned down?"

Gloria waved the scissors in the air. "Oh, no. I don't want to gawk at someone else's misfortune. It seems like courting bad luck."

Looking at the woman in the mirror, Angie gave an agreeing nod. *After giving me all these fictional answers, you must be headed for a heap of bad luck.* All Angie wanted was to get out of that salon and get as far away from Gloria as she could.

Ellie came up beside her sister and the stylist. "I'm done. I just wanted my bangs cut." She eyed Gloria suspiciously.

Gloria smiled at Ellie. "Your bangs look nice." The woman's eyes traveled to the hollow of Ellie's neck. The cabochon on the necklace that belonged to the girls' mother rested just below Ellie's collar bone.

For a few seconds, the stylist's eyes locked onto the necklace. "So pretty. Is it new?"

The intensity of Gloria's gaze startled Ellie and she took a step back. She stammered, "I've had it for a while."

"What kind of stone is it?"

Ellie's hand went to the cabochon. "I'm not sure." Something about Gloria's interest felt off and Ellie didn't want to give her any information about the necklace. "We need to get back to the house. I'll wait for you at the front desk," she told Angie.

***

WALKING BACK through town, the girls discussed Gloria's lies and seemingly strong interest in Ellie's necklace.

"It was weird." Ellie kept reaching to her neck to touch the stone. "She wouldn't take her eyes off my necklace."

"She admitted to me that she was at the common fire. The other night she told me she hadn't been on the common."

"She must have been the person I saw in the long coat." Ellie shivered. "What's she up to?"

"Gloria lied about knowing Walter Withers, too." Angie's jaw was set from her anger and disappointment. She felt betrayed. "I asked if she'd been back to Greenhill Road ... if she'd seen the burned house again. She said no, but she was there last night."

"Does she want to hurt us?" Ellie didn't wait for a response. "Why does she want to hurt us?"

Angie stopped and faced her sister. "Why was she staring at your necklace?"

"I felt weird when she was looking at it." Ellie protectively placed her hand over the stone at her neck.

"Last night you felt like you had to come to the salon with me today, but you didn't know why. It must be because we needed to notice Gloria's interest in the necklace. The necklace must be a clue." Zings of electricity thrummed through Angie's body. "Put your collar up. Cover it over." She glanced around to see if anyone was watching them and then she put her hand through Ellie's arm. They hurried down Main Street.

"Gloria lied about everything." Ellie's voice shook.

Angie thought of Professor Tyler's lie to her that morning about never being in the back garden before. Euclid knew the man had been in the yard previously. Angie's eyes narrowed. "Gloria's not the only one lying to us. We need to find out what's going on."

CHAPTER 18

When Angie and Ellie got home they busied themselves in the kitchen making vegan macaroni and cheese and a pasta Alfredo with lemon asparagus. Angie put together a garden salad and some garlic bread to go with the pasta dishes and there were small glasses of coconut ice cream with chocolate shavings and small butter cookies for dessert. When the others arrived home for dinner, they carried the food into the family room where they could speak freely and not be interrupted by B and B guests.

"This is delicious." Courtney got up from the easy chair and took a second helping from the serving dishes on the side table. "I was starving."

Euclid and Circe ate a bit of macaroni and cheese from their saucers.

Angie and Ellie told the family what had happened in Gloria's hair salon. "I'm really disgusted with Gloria," Ellie said. "I always thought she was good. Can no one be trusted?"

"I'm confused though." Courtney held her fork

in the air. "Why haven't we picked up some bad feelings when we've been around Gloria? We all get our hair cut there. How could she hide her badness and ill-intentions from us for so long? Not one of us has ever picked up anything when we're in the salon."

"Why is she lying to us?" Ellie scowled. "Why is she sneaking around the Crosswort house with Walter Withers?"

No one had an answer.

"And I caught her off guard." Angie sipped from her tea mug. "She told me before she wasn't in Sweet Cove the night of the scarecrow fires, but today she mentioned something about how the common looked when the fire was burning. She didn't catch her mistake."

Ellie unconsciously moved her hand to the white stone around her neck. "And the way she looked at my necklace. It was unnerving."

"Gloria loves jewelry though." Jenna balanced her dinner plate on her knees. "She comes into my shop a lot. She always buys a few pieces when she comes in. Maybe the necklace just caught her eye. Maybe there isn't anything sinister or peculiar about her interest in Ellie's necklace."

Ellie considered Jenna's comments and then she scrunched up her nose. "But it didn't *feel* right."

"I think we need to respect your sense of intuition." Mr. Finch said. "I believe in giving people the benefit of the doubt, but not in this case.

That woman is up to something and it involves us."

Nervous energy caused Ellie to shift around in her seat. "Why did we all dream of the mistletoe the other night?" Her voice seemed to go up an octave. "Why was my face reflected in it? What does it mean?"

Angie looked over at Finch. "You went to the library the other day to research mistletoe. What did you find out?"

"I didn't end up at the library after all. I took a detour." Finch smiled. "I decided to speak to a horticulturalist."

"Did you visit the florist shop?" Angie questioned.

"No." Circe perched on the arm of the chair that Mr. Finch was sitting in and he held a small piece of macaroni in his hand so that the black cat could nibble it. "I went to see Miss Betty."

"Oh, right." Courtney sat up with interest. "I forgot Betty has a small greenhouse behind her house. She knows all about flowers and plants."

"I had a most interesting chat with her over lunch." Finch patted the velvet fur of the cat. "She is a wealth of knowledge."

"What did you learn?" Jenna was eager to hear.

"Many of the same things that Rufus told us. The history, the cultures that held the plant in high esteem, the legends about it. Fascinating, really. Miss Betty has quite a nice library on horticulture. We spent time looking things up in her books."

"You found the things that Rufus told us?" Angie asked.

"Yes. Mistletoe has been thought to have many magical properties. The belief that kissing someone under the plant will lead to a long and happy life together is held by many cultures all over the world. The white berries contain powerful magic and can light the way when someone is lost. The plant is supposed to have the power to open all locks." Finch raised an eyebrow. "And it protects against fires."

"Huh." Courtney blinked. "That must be why it shows up each time there's a fire."

"It's not protecting against fires very well, is it?" Ellie sniffed. "We've had two fires in town in a couple of days."

Courtney cocked her head. "Well, maybe the plant *is* protecting. Maybe without it, those fires would have gone out of control, burned other things down, too."

"Good point." Angie had her index finger resting against her cheek. "Chief Martin told me that the fire at the Greenhill Road house went out of control in an oddly fast way. The fire chief thought it strange that no one noticed the fire or called it in until it was out of control." Something else came into Angie's mind. "And what about the electrical disturbance that caused the security tapes from businesses around the common to go all snowy right at the time someone would have been putting the scarecrows up and starting the fire?" Angie took a deep breath. "There seems to be some paranormal influence at work."

"I think you're right, Miss Angie." Finch furrowed his brow. "I think when I sensed the danger coming for us the other day, it felt more powerful because of the paranormal element involved."

"Oh, this is just great." Ellie stood up and started pacing. "What are we going to do?"

Courtney said, "I think we need to chat with Walter Withers some more. See if we can sense anything from him. Try to get an inkling of what he might be up to."

"I also think we need to pay attention to Professor Tyler. I've enjoyed talking with him. I thought he was a nice man." Angie bit her lower lip. "But he lied to me today. He said that this morning was the first time he'd been in the back garden, but Euclid knew he was lying."

"And we can add to all these happenings the fact that someone broke into Tom's and my house. It must all be related." Jenna shook her head. "So much deception going on. Why? What's the reason?"

"It's like the squares of a quilt." Ellie stared out the window into the dark yard. "You can only see the whole pattern once the pieces are stitched together."

"Then we'd better start stitching," Courtney said.

She glanced down at Euclid who was squished in the chair with her. "Because I get the feeling we need to figure this out pretty darned soon."

Euclid trilled his agreement.

***

ANGIE WOKE with a start and sat up, disoriented. She was aware that she'd had a nightmare, but she couldn't recall any of the details. It was like someone took an eraser and rubbed the dream out her memory. She leaned back against the pillows and tried to recall the images and how they'd made her feel.

After a minute passed, she was still unable to remember any part of her dream, but she could feel her tension draining away as she rested there breathing slowly in and out. She turned her head to the window and could see stars high in the night sky. Her eyelids felt heavy and in a few moments they shut as she drifted off to sleep.

A bang and the tinkling of glass shook Angie from her slumber. She sat up, blinking. Exhaling loudly and annoyed with her disturbed sleep, she wondered why she'd been startled awake again by another foolish dream. She wondered what they meant and why they were tormenting her. She put her head on her pillow and moved to her side trying to get comfortable when a strange smell flickered in her nostrils.

Angie jumped out of bed and stood barefoot on the wood floor listening. Another whiff of the unusual smell drifted past her. Just as she started for the bedroom door, she heard Euclid let out a howl somewhere in the house. Angie's heart pounded double-time and she broke into a run.

On the second floor landing, she paused.

Euclid shrieked again and Angie flicked on the lights and flew down the staircase to find the orange cat standing over some object on the foyer rug. Circe let out a cry near the front door. Angie could see the door was slightly ajar. She whirled around trying to see if someone was in the house. She looked at Euclid. "Is someone inside?"

The cat just stared at her with his big green eyes.

"I'll take that as a no."

Courtney leaned over the railing of the second floor landing. "What's going on down there?"

Angie lifted her face. "I think someone broke in."

Courtney rushed down the stairs. "Why do you think someone broke in?" She spotted the door pushed open a few inches. Cool air streamed into the foyer. "Oh." She scrunched up her nose. "What stinks?" She saw Euclid standing next to something. "What's that on the floor?"

Angie and Courtney took a few steps forward.

Courtney crouched. "It looks like...." She stood up fast. "Is that a homemade firebomb?"

Angie's mouth dropped open. "Is it going to go

off?"

"I'm sure that was the plan." Courtney edged closer and peered at the thing. "I bet it's a dud and didn't ignite like it was supposed to."

"How do you know what it is?" Angie looked pale.

"I watch crime shows, Sis."

Angie stepped to the front door. "Someone broke the window in the door. They must have opened it and tossed that thing in here." Angie put her hands on her hips. "Thank heavens it didn't go off. I'm going to call the police." Before pushing the numbers on the phone, she remembered that a police car was parked in front of the house at night so she stepped out on the porch to signal to the officer.

Ellie appeared on the landing looking down with bleary eyes. "What are you doing?"

Courtney explained what had happened and Ellie had to grip the banister as she slid to sitting position on the top step. She pressed her hand to her eyes. Just as she was about to dissolve into tears from her fear and worry, Ellie's face hardened and she sucked in a long, slow breath. She lifted her face, her eyes flashing like steel. "You aren't going to beat us," she whispered. "Whoever you are."

CHAPTER 19

Courtney went up to check that Ellie was okay and she was glad to see that her sister had recovered from the momentary shock. She glanced to the stairs that led to the third floor. "Is Sleeping Beauty awake? That girl can sleep through anything."

The sisters always teased Jenna that she wouldn't wake up even if an atom bomb went off in the house. Courtney climbed the staircase to the third floor to wake Jenna and on the way back down, one of the B and B guests poked a head out of their door.

"Is there a problem?" An older man stood just inside his room, his wife behind him looking over his shoulder.

"Just a fire bomb." Courtney headed for the first floor. "But it didn't go off."

Ellie glared at her sister. "Don't frighten the guests." She stood up and went over to speak to the man to reassure him. "It was just a prank. Everything's fine, but we've made a call to the police for them to check things out. Why don't we all head down to our family room at the back of the house until the police arrive? We'll set out some treats and drinks for everyone." Ellie smiled reassuringly.

Jenna appeared on the landing, her hair tousled from sleep. She tied the belt of her robe around her waist. "What's going on? Someone threw a firebomb into the house?" She rubbed the sleep from her eyes and yawned.

"You don't seem very concerned." Ellie stared at her sister.

Jenna pushed her hair back from her face. "Courtney said it was no big deal."

Ellie shook her head. "Will you help me gather the guests and herd them into the family room? No one should stay in their rooms until the police give us the all clear."

Jenna and Ellie moved from room to room to rouse the guests.

Before long, someone knocked on the door. It was Officer Talbot. "I just talked with the officer on duty outside. I've contacted Chief Martin. He's on his way." Talbot asked Angie to explain what had happened. While she was telling him, he and the other officer carefully checked the object on the foyer floor. "Looks like a homemade incendiary device." Talbot bent down to have a closer look. "Some of the liquid is leaking out. You're lucky this thing didn't go off. It would have caused a lot of damage."

Angie frowned. She had her arms wrapped around herself. "Someone must be very disappointed." Suddenly she looked at Courtney with wide eyes, grabbed her phone, and punched numbers into it. "Mr. Finch. He might be a target as well."

Courtney didn't wait to hear another word. She and Officer Talbot raced out of the house heading for Mr. Finch's place with Circe and Euclid chasing after them.

After several rings, a sleepy-sounding Finch answered his phone, and Angie sank onto one of the dining chairs, relief flooding her body. She told the older man what had happened and that Courtney and Officer Talbot were on their way to his house to check things out.

Chief Martin strode through the front door, his eyes darting around taking everything in. His face softened when he saw Angie. "You okay?"

She nodded and stood up. "Never a dull moment."

"A technician is on his way to look this over and remove it. We'll check it out for fingerprints and what not." The chief stepped across the room to confer with the other officer about the front door's broken glass and the condition of the incendiary device. He decided there was no need to evacuate the premises, but that everyone should stay at the back of the house until the thing had been removed.

"Ellie and Jenna have moved the guests to the

family room," Angie told the chief. "Tom's on his way over to close up the broken window."

"Why don't you join the others in the family room? I'll let you know when the coast is clear."

Courtney walked into the foyer with the cats next to her. Her eyes were twinkling. She leaned towards Angie as the two of them headed for the hallway. "Guess what? It seems Mr. Finch has an overnight guest."

Angie's eyebrows shot up and a smile crept over her lips. The cats trilled.

"Betty came to the door with him. You should have seen him blush." Courtney chuckled as they went to the kitchen to help prepare more snacks and treats for the inconvenienced guests. "Everything was okay. If I knew Betty was there with Mr. Finch, I wouldn't have bothered to go check on him." Courtney was only half-kidding when she said, "If anyone ever tried to hurt Mr. Finch, I have no doubt they would have to go through Betty first. Mr. Finch has his own personal bodyguard."

Ellie stood at the counter placing a pot of coffee and a silver tea pot onto a tray along with a sugar bowl and creamer. Her sisters could see the anger on Ellie's face as she faced them. "Everyone is present and accounted for except for one of the guests."

Angie was about to ask which one when she caught herself. "Oh."

Courtney was steaming. "Could the missing person be Mr. Walter Withers?"

Ellie lifted the tray. "Chief Martin might want to have a talk with the gentleman about his whereabouts this evening."

"Is Professor Tyler in the family room?" Angie asked.

"Yes." Ellie spoke over her shoulder as she headed for the hall. "He was asleep in the sunroom. He said he was restless and came downstairs to read. He didn't hear anything because he'd fallen asleep in the chair."

***

COURTNEY, ANGIE, and Jenna sat at the round table next to the fireplace in the jewelry room bent over mats with silver findings and different colored glass beads spread out between them. It was a cool night and they thought it would be nice to have a fire going while they worked putting together Jenna's necklace designs, but with all the fire trouble in town recently, Jenna was reluctant to light the logs.

"We can't let some evil creep keep us from enjoying ourselves." Courtney strung a blue and white bead on the wire. "Let's just light it."

Angie got up and started the fire and once it kicked in with a lovely blaze going, Jenna agreed that it made the room cozy and was glad that

Courtney had convinced them. Euclid and Circe curled up on the rug in front of the fireplace.

Suddenly, Courtney grew quiet and Angie asked her what was wrong.

"Rufus is leaving in three days."

Angie and Jenna could see the light from the fire reflecting off their youngest sister's teary blue eyes.

"We've talked about me going to England so we can stay together while he finishes his studies."

Euclid raised his head and released a soft, low hiss. Jenna froze in place with her crimping tool suspended in mid-air. Angie's heart clenched thinking of Courtney leaving the family to move to England, but she hid her feelings. "You love each other. You should be together."

"But I just started the business with Mr. Finch and I don't want to leave all of you." Courtney let out a sigh. "I don't know what to do."

Jenna swallowed hard. "Keep thinking about it. Do what you think is best." She put her hand on her sister's arm. "We want you to be happy."

Just as Courtney was about to say thank you, Jenna added, "Even if what you do makes *us* unhappy."

Courtney bopped her on the shoulder. "Thanks a lot."

"I had to lighten the mood." Jenna smiled. "Honestly, you know we support whatever you want to do."

Angie got in on the act. "Even if we think you're

wrong."

Courtney groaned. "You two are horrible sisters."

The door to the jewelry room opened and Ellie poked her head in. "Look who I found lurking on the front porch."

Rufus came into the room and Ellie returned to the kitchen. He looked handsome with the front of his light brown hair hanging over his forehead and his bright blue eyes shining at Courtney. Leaning down, he touched her cheek and kissed her on top of the head. He sank into the sofa next to the desks and the two cats walked over, jumped up, and settled against him purring.

"I'm almost finished with this piece, and then we can go." Courtney put the last bead on the necklace she was working on. She looked up at Angie and Jenna. "I forgot to tell you. Jack's having a little going-away get-together for Rufus at the law office. He's going to have cake and coffee and tea. He invited all of us." She told her sisters when the gathering would be and they said they'd love to come.

Rufus said, "Did Chief Martin find out anything about your firebug of last night?"

Angie leaned over the necklace she was working on. "No prints were found, nothing on the device and nothing on the front door."

"Not much to go on then." Rufus watched Courtney as she added the clasp to the jewelry piece. "I suppose it could be unrelated to the fires in town."

Three pairs of eyes turned and stared at him.

He modified his statement. "Or it was absolutely related to the fires in town."

"Too bad we don't have a security camera on the front of the house." Courtney placed the necklace she had just finished into a jewelry box, stood up, and picked up her sweater from the back of her chair.

"Tom wants to install one on the porch roof." Angie smiled. "We keep him busy around here."

Rufus extricated himself from the cats and got up from the sofa. He and Courtney had made plans to see a movie at the theatre in the center of town.

"Too bad I didn't come by the house just a few minutes later." Rufus took Courtney's hand.

Angie looked up. "What do you mean?"

"Last night. I was working late in my apartment."

"He's a night owl," Courtney told them.

"I was feeling antsy and wasn't ready to sleep, so I went for a run."

"You went for a run in the middle of the night?" Jenna made a face thinking how that would be the last thing she would ever want to do.

Rufus nodded. "It's nice out then, peaceful. I usually run down Main Street and turn onto your street. I go right by your house, head down to the beach, and make a loop up Willow Street."

"Was the police car out front when you went by?" Angie asked.

"Yes, but no one was in it."

"The officer must have been walking around the house," Jenna noted.

"You didn't see anyone suspicious?" Angie set her tool on the table.

Rufus shrugged. "Like I said, if I was a few minutes later I would have caught the guy in the act."

"Did you notice a car go by or someone walking around?" Jenna knew Rufus probably wouldn't have paid attention to anyone nearby since he had no reason to suspect wrong-doing about to occur.

"No one dangerous looking." He and Courtney headed for the door. "Unless you count an old lady in a dark coat standing across the street."

CHAPTER 20

Angie's eyes bugged out and Jenna's mouth dropped open.

"An old lady?" Angie stood up.

"Where?" Jenna's eyes bored into the young man.

A surprised look washed over Rufus's face. "She was standing across from your house. I thought she must have been waiting for a ride. I didn't pay much attention to her." He took a look at Courtney and then shifted his gaze back to the sisters. "You think an old lady wanted to burn your house down?"

"What did she look like?" Angie stepped around from behind the table.

"Um." Rufus thought back on the night. "She had on a dark coat."

"How long was the coat?" Jenna turned the palm of her hand horizontal to the floor and held it to her knee and then to mid-calf. "Here?"

"I think it was below the knee." Rufus didn't sound positive. "Maybe?"

"Why did you call her an *old* lady?" Angie wondered what it was about the person that caused Rufus to think she was old.

"She had grayish hair, sort of whitish. Like I said, I didn't really pay attention. I just ran by."

"Was she wearing a hood?" Jenna asked.

Rufus shook his head. "No hood."

Angie thought there was a possibility it could be Mrs. Crosswort. "Did she seem frail, sickly?"

"Ahh...." Rufus looked perplexed.

Courtney took her boyfriend's arm. "I don't think Rufus could determine that in the split second he ran past. It was dark."

"Sorry that I didn't see more," Rufus said as he and Courtney left the room.

Angie and Jenna stared at each other.

"Was it Angelina Crosswort?" Angie sat back down.

"Or was it Gloria?" Jenna walked over to the sofa and stretched out. "My head is spinning. Who would have thought Rufus would be out at that time of night and happen to see whoever broke in here?"

"I guess there's a chance the woman he saw didn't have anything to do with it." Angie put her chin in her hand.

"Really?" Jenna made a face. "That woman must have been watching the house for a while, waiting for the officer to do his walk around the back. As soon as he was out of sight, she sprang into action and was gone before he came around front. I bet she'd watched him on more than one occasion to find out his pattern, how much time it took to do his round."

A cloud settled over Angie's face. "Something doesn't seem right. Something feels off."

Before the conversation could continue, Ellie came into the room. "Can you fix my necklace?"

"What's wrong with it?"

Ellie handed it to Jenna. "The chain was caught in my hair and when I tugged on it, the latch got distorted."

Jenna placed the necklace on the felt mat in front of her and adjusted the lamp to shine on it. She peered at the clasp and then picked up one of her tools.

Ellie yawned. "I have to go clean up the carriage house apartment."

"Why?" Angie picked up some beads and went back to working on a necklace.

"Professor Tyler wants to stay longer. He asked if he might move into one of the apartments. He'd like to do some cooking instead of eating out so often."

"He's planning to stay longer?" Angie slipped a silver crimp bead along the jewelry wire.

"He wants to rent the apartment for at least another month." Ellie yawned. "I'm exhausted from last night." The girls were up for hours settling the guests and talking things over after the police had finished inspecting the house and removing the firebomb. None of them had been able to return to sleep after the nighttime disturbance.

"I'll help you get the apartment ready." Angie held up the necklace she'd been working on for her sister's approval.

"Looks great," Jenna said. After some minor adjustments on Ellie's piece, she tried the clasp. "It's fine now." Jenna held it up to her neck. "This would look pretty with my new shirt."

"Hand it over, you." Ellie held out her hand. "Maybe I'll let you borrow it someday."

Jenna dropped the necklace into her sister's hand and Ellie attached it around her neck. The white stone seemed to shimmer. Angie admired the gem and the way the fire reflected off of it. Suddenly she sat up straight. "Can I see the necklace?"

"Why?" Ellie thought her sister might be about to pull a prank on her.

"I'll give it right back." Angie could feel her pulse quicken and her blood thrum through her veins.

Ellie unclasped the silver chain and passed the piece to her sister. Angie looked down at the necklace as she held it up to her throat, and then handed it to Jenna. "Hold it up again."

Lifting it to her neck, Jenna narrowed her eyes trying to imagine what her twin sister was up to.

Angie leaned across the table, intent on the

white stone. "Now, hand it to Ellie again."

Ellie rolled her eyes and put the necklace back on. "Can I keep it this time?"

Angie sat back in her chair, her eyes still glued to the piece of jewelry around Ellie's neck. "That stone."

Ellie and Jenna made eye contact with one another.

"What about it?" Jenna asked.

"It only glows when Ellie wears it."

The three girls handed the necklace around to each other a few more times to corroborate Angie's statement.

"At first I thought it was just the fire reflecting off the stone, but when Jenna held it up, the white of the stone looked opaque, almost dull, and it didn't shine." Angie fiddled with one of the jewelry tools. "But when Ellie wears it, the stone seems to sparkle and swim in the light. It shimmers. It almost comes alive."

"Huh." Ellie shook her head, her fingers stroking the white cabochon. "But, why?"

"It was Mom's," Jenna said. "You look the most like her. She didn't want anything to do with powers, either. You're just like her. The stone wants to be with you."

Ellie's face drooped and she swallowed hard. "But, why?" she asked again. "Why does it shimmer when I have it on? What's it all about?"

Jenna glanced across the room to the window

sill where she kept the jar of sea glass that her Nana had given her. "I wish Nana was here. I bet she could tell us about the stone."

"The dreams." Angie looked over at Ellie. "We saw your reflection in the white berries of the mistletoe in all of our dreams. Somehow the stone in the necklace and the mistletoe … and you, must all fit together."

Ellie stood up, her hands shaking. She started to pace around the room. The cats watched her back and forth movement. "Remember how Gloria looked at the necklace? It made me feel strange." Ellie made eye contact with Angie. "Well, this morning when you were in the walk-in freezer, I came into the bake shop to get a chocolate croissant for my favorite guest." She made a face thinking of Walter Withers. "Louisa was busy ringing people up and she asked me to bring the Crossworts their coffee. When I set the mugs on their table, their eyes went right to my necklace. I was bent over and the necklace was hanging forward. Mrs. Crosswort reached out and touched it." Ellie's lips were tight. "I thought she had such a nerve. It startled me. I practically jumped back."

"They're odd people. No social skills." Jenna shook her head.

"I didn't like it, not at all." Clutching a strand of her hair, Ellie braided and unbraided it. "Maybe I should put the necklace back in the box until I know what's going on." She stopped in mid-step.

"I don't want to do anything wrong." Turning quickly, she hurried to the door. "That's what I'm going to do."

They heard Ellie's heels clicking away on the wood floor of the hall. "Do you think she should put it back in the box?" Angie asked.

"Who knows? It is strange that Gloria and Mrs. Crossword reacted in such a weird way when they spotted the necklace." Jenna picked up a red gemstone from the table and held it up to the firelight admiring the color. "You think the necklace has something to do with the mistletoe?"

"Wait a minute." Angie leaned forward. "How long ago did Ellie find the box of Mom's things?"

"Well, the box has been in the carriage house since we all moved here. Ellie just fished it out recently though. Why?"

"The necklace was in that white leather box. It must have been in there since Mom died."

"What are you getting at?" Jenna had the feeling that her sister was on to something.

Angie felt the low rhythmic beating in her blood. "When did Ellie open the box? Is it a coincidence that she found that necklace at the same time someone started to threaten us?"

Euclid sat up on the sofa and made a soft clicking sound like when he saw birds through the window and wanted to hunt them.

Jenna's lips parted like she was going to speak. She paused trying to make sense of the things that had happened over the past week. "Ellie opened the box around the same time that we noticed the mistletoe in the tree." Her heart rate quickened. "The Crossworts showed up then, too, and Walter Withers."

Angie's voice shook. "Were those people drawn here because Ellie opened the box?"

"It doesn't seem like coincidence, does it?" Jenna raised her eyes to her sister. "Have the Crossworts been coming into the bake shop every morning?"

Angie gave a nod. "Except for one day, they're in there like clockwork. The woman looks worse every day." She looked across the room, thinking, something picking at her mind. "Professor Tyler comes in every morning, too. It's funny though, the Crossworts always seem to leave just before the professor arrives." Angie gave a little shrug. The bits of information swirled around like crisp autumn leaves caught in a breeze, not easy to pin down or to put in order.

Circe moved from the cushion to the arm of the sofa, her green eyes flashing.

"Maybe putting the necklace away for a while will settle things down." Angie hoped so.

Ellie came back into the room carrying the white leather box. She'd overheard Angie's comment. "I doubt putting the necklace away will stop whoever wants to hurt us."

"It feels like things are escalating." Jenna picked

up the completed jewelry pieces and carried them to the long work table where she would pack them for shipping. "I don't think putting the necklace away can put the brakes on the person who's threatening us."

Angie rubbed her index finger over the small box. Little zips of electricity bit the tip of her finger. She pressed on it and felt the unusual hardness of the box. Lifting it, she turned it in different directions continuing to press here and there. "This isn't a normal box." She slid it across the tabletop for Jenna to inspect it. Euclid and Circe jumped on the table to sniff the box.

"It's really hard ... and heavy. What's it made of? Lead?" Jenna joked.

Angie started to chuckle and then stopped. "Lead."

"What's wrong with lead?" Ellie glanced from sister to sister.

"Nothing," Angie said. "It's very dense, it's used to protect against gamma rays and against radiation in x-rays. Technicians wear lead aprons or shields when they x-ray someone." Angie had a scientific background having graduated from MIT.

"That necklace is radioactive?" Ellie stepped away from the table.

"No." Angie picked up the white box. "The lead is keeping the white stone's energy *inside* the box."

Jenna's eyes narrowed and she smiled. "That way no one knows where it is. But, if the necklace

171

is taken out of the box, then some people can sense where it is ... and come after it."

The corners of Angie's mouth turned up. "Exactly."

The two cats trilled.

CHAPTER 21

Angie locked the door of the bake shop, stretched and yawned. It had been another busy day and she was feeling exhausted. She hadn't been sleeping well the past few nights. She was always listening for any sound that might indicate someone trying to break into the house. Fitful dreams and staying awake trying to piece clues together added to her fatigue.

"What's cookin,' Sis?" Courtney came in and opened the refrigerator. "Jenna wants a latte and there isn't any milk in the house fridge."

"There's plenty in there. Take some into the house." Angie wiped down the countertop and then removed her apron and placed it in the laundry bin. "Are you doing okay?"

Courtney knew what she meant. Rufus was leaving for England in two days. She gave Angie a wistful smile. "I'm okay. I'm trying to keep busy at all times."

Angie flicked off the light in the bake shop and followed her sister into the house. Mr. Finch sat at the kitchen table reading the newspaper with Circe sitting beside him. He looked up when the girls came in.

"What's wrong, Miss Angie?"

Angie sank into the chair opposite Finch. "I'm feeling uneasy." She made a face. "All the time."

Courtney put two jugs of milk onto the counter, reached for a cup, and made Jenna's latte. "Maybe it's because of your creepy customers."

"They didn't come in today."

Courtney looked over her shoulder. "That's unusual, isn't it?"

"They've only missed one other day besides today."

Courtney put the cup on a saucer and headed for the hall to deliver the drink to Jenna. "The Crossworts bother you when they come into the bake shop and they bother you when they don't. You can't win."

Angie looked at Mr. Finch. "I don't think the Crossworts are the cause of what's bothering me. They're not the whole reason anyway."

Finch folded the newspaper and pushed it to the side of the table. He made eye contact with Angie, but didn't say anything. Circe rubbed her cheek against the man's hand and he obliged by scratching her. After a few moments, Finch said, "I think your unease will be gone soon."

"Will the outcome be good or bad?"

"Unknown." Finch continued to scratch the cat's

cheek.

"Someone's about to make a move?"

"I think so, yes."

A noise at the doorway made them both look across the room. Ellie stood at the threshold staring at them. Her face looked ghostly pale. "Why do I always walk in on these kinds of conversations?" She stepped into the kitchen and let out a sigh. "I'm going to busy myself by starting dinner."

"What are you going to make? I'll help." Angie pushed herself out of the chair.

Ellie took some ingredients out of the refrigerator. "Why don't you go for a run instead?"

Angie blinked. "Why?"

Ellie straightened up, her hand still on the fridge door. "I don't know why." Her cheeks tinged pink. She stammered trying to cover her fluster. "You, ah, you haven't exercised for days, ever since these fires started happening. It might do you good."

Angie looked at Mr. Finch and he raised an eyebrow. She cocked her head and asked Ellie, "Is this one of your things like when you say something about Chief Martin and then he calls? Do you have some feeling that I should go for a run?"

"No." Ellie replied too fast which made Angie think that the real answer was yes.

"Okay. I want to talk to the chief anyway so maybe I'll jog down to the police station." Angie started for the hallway to go to her room to change into running clothes. "Tomorrow afternoon, I'm going to go see Francine's new stained glass store in the center of town. I saw her this morning in the bake shop. She said her place is coming out really nice and she invited us all to come by. Her grandmother is helping her and Francine said she used to know Nana. She'd like to meet us."

Mr. Finch told Angie that perhaps it might be wise if he stayed at the Victorian to keep an eye on things while the girls visited the stained glass store and met Francine's grandmother. The family was trying to have at least one person at home at all times in case trouble reared its head. Ellie wanted to go along to Francine's, so they set a time.

Angie headed out of the kitchen. "I'll ask Jenna and Courtney to come, too."

✳✳✳

AS SHE ran down Main Street, Angie had to admit that the exercise was doing her good. The late afternoon was clear and cool and the sun was low on the horizon painting strips of pink and violet against the darkening blue sky. Angie waved to acquaintances as she made her was down the road and she glanced into shop windows as she passed. The stores and restaurants had colorful mums and small pumpkins in their window boxes and at their entrances. Some store windows had displays of black cats and ghosts set beside pumpkins and cornstalks. A smile played over Angie's lips. She loved the festive atmosphere in town and the fall weather and its hint of the coming holiday season.

By the time she reached the police station, Angie's muscles and lungs were burning from the exertion, but she had to admit that running had drained the tension from her body. Climbing the steps to the station, she used her forearm to wipe the sweat off her brow. Inside she was greeted by Officer Talbot and led to Chief Martin's small, spare office.

"Angie." The chief looked up and smiled. "I was just going to text you."

Hope filled her chest. "You have a lead?" She sat in the metal chair in front of the chief's desk.

A small one. Maybe." Chief Martin twirled a pencil between his fingers. "The techs have been working on the security camera footage."

"I thought the tapes were useless from the electrical blip or whatever it was."

"The techs have been able to filter out some of the static and blur. Somewhat." The chief leaned back in his well-worn, squeaky chair. "I haven't seen it yet, but I'm told you can make out a form moving about on the common. I assume the person is setting up the scarecrows. They're sending the photos over either tonight or tomorrow morning. I'll make copies and you and your sisters and Mr. Finch can take a look. I'll drop them off at the house."

Angie's eyes were wide. "That's good. That's something." She nodded with enthusiasm. "Anything might help."

"Anything new on your end?" The chief raised an eyebrow.

Angie realized he was hoping she'd dropped in with some bit of information. "I was just wondering if there were any new clues." She bit her lip. "There is something though." She told the chief about the necklace and certain people's expressions of interest in it. "Gloria's eyes bugged out when she saw it and Mrs. Crosswort had the nerve to actually reach out and touch it. Ellie was really taken aback." She explained their suspicion that the white stone gave off energy of some sort and that being in its lead box kept the energy inside.

Chief Martin's face was blank and he blinked a few times before saying anything. Even though he'd worked with the girls' Nana on many cases and accepted the Roseland's abilities, he was often still surprised by and unsure of how to address their skills. "Well, that's, um, interesting."

Angie couldn't help chuckling. "Who knows if there's any connection between the necklace and what's been going on. We're probably just clutching at straws."

They chatted about other aspects of the case and other unrelated things going on in town. Angie started to shiver from the cold, wet sweat clinging to her skin. "I'd better head home." She stood up and went to the door, but hesitated for a moment. She turned to the chief. "Mr. Finch senses that someone is about to make another move. We should be on guard."

The chief's cheek muscle twitched as a grave expression crossed over his face. "Be careful."

Angie nodded. "You, too." A quick shudder ran down her back, but the cold sweat on her skin wasn't the cause.

***

RUNNING BACK up the street, a heavy sense of fatigue came over Angie, but she pressed on hoping she would get a second wind if she kept going. She knew her sense of desperation over the case was mixed in with her physical weariness and the combination was sapping her energy. Her breathing was labored and her leg muscles were on fire. She watched the people and tourists on the sidewalks as she passed trying to distract herself from her pain. The gift shops and restaurant buildings cast long shadows and, here and there, the streetlamps started to glow.

Although Angie felt it was cheating, she decided that instead of slowing to a walk, she would keep running, but would take a side street home that would cut off some of the distance she'd have to cover if she remained on the main street. She decided it was a decent compromise. Plodding along with heavy legs, she promised herself to get back into a regular exercise routine and to stop making excuses.

Angie hadn't been on this street for a while and she saw several shops that she enjoyed browsing through in the past. There was one that sold beautiful handmade Irish sweaters and she'd thought of getting one for Ellie for Christmas. She made a mental note to visit the shop soon. Up ahead, coming down the sidewalk towards her, an older couple weaved around some tourists, and Angie glanced away. Something about them caused her to look again and her heart pounded as she ran by. Halting in her tracks, she whirled around to see the couple step into an old car and drive away. Angie stood on the side of the street with her mouth open.

She was sure that the couple who had hurried along the sidewalk past her was the Crossworts, but Mrs. Crosswort looked completely different. She no longer looked sickly. Her skin was rosy and her eyes were bright. The woman's posture was upright and she moved with vigor, her step light and easy.

Angie shook herself. *It couldn't have been Mrs. Crosswort. Maybe it was her sister or some other relative who resembled the woman.* Turning away and breaking into a run, she took one more look back over her shoulder.

180

CHAPTER 22

Ellie stood in the foyer and called up the stairs. "Are you coming?"

Jenna hurried across the landing and down the stairs to the first floor. She lifted her long brown hair off her shoulders and put it into a ponytail.

While she was waiting for the others, Angie sat at the dining table going over the monthly figures for her shop. Euclid and Circe watched her from high on the China cabinet.

"You ready, Angie?" Ellie pulled a red and white cardigan over her head. "Where's Courtney?"

"I'm right here." Courtney came into the foyer from the hall. "I was putting a box of summer clothes in the carriage house storage area." She had her index finger stuck in the back of a baseball cap and swung it back and forth. "Does this belong to one of your guests? I found it outside."

Ellie took it. It had an "NY" insignia embroidered on the front. "A Yankees hat?"

Euclid gave a hiss.

"Really." Courtney winked at the orange cat.

"Who'd wear a New York Yankees hat in Massachusetts?"

"I don't recognize it. I haven't noticed a guest wearing it." Ellie placed the cap on the foyer table.

"I told Mr. Finch that we're leaving." Courtney picked up her wallet. "He's in the family room watching a crime show."

The two cats jumped off the China cabinet and raced down the hall to find Mr. Finch.

Angie closed her ledger and stood up. "Okay, let's go."

The sisters headed up Beach Street to the center of town. They waved at the employees working inside the candy store as they walked past on their way to Francine's new shop. As they strolled, Angie told the girls about running past the Crossworts last evening and how she thought the woman was Mrs. Crosswort, but must have been mistaken since the person seemed so vigorous and healthy.

"It must be a relative of hers," Ellie noted. "Unless Mrs. Crosswort had some miraculous recovery."

Angie agreed, but a skitter of unease ran over her skin.

"Oh, look." Courtney pointed. "I love Francine's new sign."

The wooden sign was similar to the one above the candy shop. "She asked me and Mr. Finch if she could have the name of the person who did ours. It came out great."

Francine was still preparing the space she had leased and wouldn't open until just before Thanksgiving. It wasn't the best time to open a new shop in a coastal town, but she hoped December visitors to Sweet Cove would make some Christmas purchases and she still had a booming online business.

Ellie knocked and opened the front door. The girls stepped in and Francine greeted them. Her shoulder length blonde hair swung over her shoulders and her bright blue eyes sparkled as she gave each sister a hug.

"Wow. What you've done in here is amazing." Courtney turned in a circle looking at the space that used to house a sandwich shop. "It looks so classy and elegant now."

Jenna agreed. "You'd never know it was the same shop."

A short, slender white-haired woman came out of the back room carrying a can of paint. She had the same wide, friendly blue eyes as Francine. "It's the Roseland girls." A welcoming smile spread over her face.

Francine had told the sisters that her grandmother was over ninety years old and they were surprised by the woman's vitality, thinking that she could easily pass for someone in her early seventies.

Francine made introductions. "This is my grandmother, Marilyn DuBois. She lived in Sweet

Cove for many years. Now she lives in Silver Cove." Silver Cove was an artist enclave a few miles north of the town of Sweet Cove.

"You each resemble your grandmother. I'd know you anywhere." Marilyn shook hands with the sisters.

Francine showed them around pointing out where display cases would be set up and where shelves were going to be placed. "I'm going to put a table right here so people can watch while I work."

Marilyn led the girls into the back room. "Francine is going to have work stations set up on this side, there are supply cabinets going over there, and this section is a place to have lunch or a snack or relax for a bit while on a break." A half-wall had been built to separate the break area from the work section of the space. There were two leather sofas, a round table with four chairs, and a mini-kitchen with a refrigerator and microwave.

Courtney ran her hand over one of the light gray leather sofas. "This is great. Maybe I'll quit the candy store and apply to work for you."

Francine and Marilyn laughed. "I see you have your Nana's sense of humor," Marilyn said.

The girls were invited to sit and Francine told them her plans for the store. "Let's have some tea or coffee." She hurried to the counter to prepare beverages and carried them over to the coffee table with a basket of butter cookies. When everyone was settled nibbling cookies and sipping drinks, Marilyn

184

and the girls discussed Nana.

"I met your Nana at a town function many years ago. I liked Virginia immediately. She was such a great conversationalist, friendly, kind, so involved in the town. We became good friends."

The sisters asked questions about Nana and Marilyn provided them with funny stories that had them all chuckling. Marilyn smiled at Jenna. "I hear you and your husband-to-be have purchased the Stenmark place. Best wishes on your engagement."

Jenna's eyes widened. "Do you know the house?"

"Oh yes, its two doors down from the Victorian."

"Why is it called the Stenmark place? Is that a previous owner?" Jenna asked.

"Katrina Stenmark owned the house a long time ago. Your Nana and I were friends of hers. She inherited the house from her grandparents and lived there with her husband and son. They passed away, unfortunately, and Katrina didn't have any living relatives so when she died, the ownership of the place was in question. It took years and years for the town to claim the house and by then it had fallen into such disrepair. I'm sure Katrina would be thrilled to know it's yours now."

Francine's phone buzzed and she took the call in the front room. She returned with a frown on her face. "I have to hurry over to the bank. There's a mix-up with my signature missing from one of the lease agreements and they need it right away. I'll only be a few minutes." She apologized and invited the sisters to stay until she got back as she was hoping to show them some new designs she had in mind for stained glass windows and lamps. She grabbed her purse and hurried away.

"Let me refill your drinks." Marilyn was about to stand, but Jenna and Courtney insisted on taking care of refreshing the beverages.

Marilyn looked at Ellie. "You look just like your mother."

Ellie nodded. Her cheeks flushed and as she shifted in her seat self-consciously her foot kicked over her unzipped purse and some of the contents spilled onto the floor. "Oh." She bent to pick up her things. "I never zip the top. Everything's always tumbling out."

Angie's eyes widened when she saw the white leather jewelry box on the floor. A zap of electricity flashed through her veins and when she looked across to where Courtney was sitting, she could tell her youngest sister had the same feeling. Courtney tilted her head and gave a little shrug.

Angie flicked her eyes to Marilyn just in time to see the look of surprise and alarm on the woman's face when she spotted the white box. Marilyn, open-mouthed, looked at Angie and when their eyes met, it was like a bright light flashed in Angie's head. She blinked hard several times and shook her shoulders.

Marilyn put her hand to her temple and shifted her gaze to the white box that was now in Ellie's hand. Ellie slid it into her purse and looked up.

In a soft voice, Marilyn said, "Your Nana had a box like that."

Angie's heart skipped a beat. "She did?" The girls hadn't realized that the necklace in the white box had belonged to their Nana and that their mom had inherited it when Nana passed away.

Marilyn nodded. Her face looked pale.

"What did she have in it?" Courtney asked.

"A necklace." Marilyn's voice could barely be heard.

Angie wasn't sure if Marilyn was friend or foe, but she couldn't ignore that this woman knew the box. She decided to pursue the subject. "What did the necklace look like?"

Marilyn started to ask something. She stopped. "It was a long time ago."

Angie knew the woman was pretending not to remember. "Marilyn, do you know something about the necklace? Because if you do, we could use your help."

Marilyn glanced to the front room, seemed to hesitate, and then made a decision. She spoke in a hurried voice. "The box belonged to Katrina Stenmark."

Surprise passed over the sisters' faces. Jenna's mouth dropped open.

"Katrina gave it to your grandmother for

safekeeping." Marilyn looked to the front room again and Angie assumed that she didn't want her granddaughter to return and hear what she was saying.

"Why did she give it to Nana?" Courtney asked.

"I don't know why." Marilyn's lips tightened into thin lines. "That's the truth. I do know that Katrina told your grandmother to keep it safe and to leave the necklace in the box."

"Did Nana ever wear it?" Angie watched the woman's face closely.

"Not that I ever saw."

"Do you know why it had to be kept in the box?" Ellie looked like she wanted to run from the room.

Marilyn shook her head vigorously. Her eyes narrowed and just as Francine opened the shop door and entered the front room, Marilyn whispered, "I don't know why it was supposed to stay in the box, but I do know that Katrina Stenmark gave her life for that necklace."

Ellie slipped to the floor in a faint.

CHAPTER 23

The sisters stayed up late telling Mr. Finch and the cats what they'd learned from Francine's grandmother about the white stone necklace. Ellie had an egg on the side of her head from hitting the floor when she fainted.

"I wish you were there with us so you could have heard it all first-hand." Angie stretched out on one of the sofas with her legs over Jenna's lap.

Mr. Finch was slowly stroking Circe's fur as he pondered the stunning information. "It's a pity that Mrs. DuBois didn't have many details."

Jenna said, "Marilyn told us that Nana didn't want to share any unnecessary details with her for safety's sake. The less Marilyn knew, the better it would be for her."

"It was pretty clear that Marilyn didn't want Francine to know anything about the necklace." Courtney scratched Euclid's cheeks. The big cat took up most of the chair they were sitting in.

There weren't any cold compresses in the house, so Ellie held a bag of frozen peas against the side of her head. "My head started buzzing when Mrs. DuBois told us that Katrina Stenmark died because of the necklace. I don't remember falling out of the chair."

Courtney smiled. "You hit the floor like a ton of bricks." She winked at Mr. Finch. "We told Francine that Ellie has low blood sugar and gets woozy sometimes."

"Clever." When Finch paused his scratching of the black cat, she nudged his hand with her nose to encourage more patting. "Why did you have the necklace with you? I thought you'd put it away."

A sheepish expression passed over Ellie's face. "I like the necklace. It makes me feel close to Mom. I knew it had to stay in the box, but I wanted it close to me. I should have left it at home."

"It was good that you had it in your bag, otherwise we wouldn't have learned what Marilyn knew," Angie said.

"So, you found out that the necklace is so important that Katrina Stenmark died keeping it safe." Mr. Finch recapped what they'd learned. "Your Nana probably knew why it was important, but did not share the reason with Mrs. DuBois. Your Nana may not have shared this information with your mother, either. It seems clear that the necklace needs to stay in its box."

Angie swung her legs over the side of the sofa and sat up, a serious expression causing lines to crease her forehead. "Ellie found the necklace in

Mom's stuff right before all the trouble started in town. This is going to sound nuts, but when Ellie opened the white box I think people who know about the necklace can sense where it is."

Ellie shifted uncomfortable in her seat.

Courtney looked excited. "Like a beacon. The necklace's energy gets released and some people can feel it. The person who set the fires knows we have it and he wants it."

"Why was there a fire near the Crossworts house then?" Ellie winced when she adjusted the position of the frozen pea bag against her head.

No one could answer that.

Something about the Crossworts picked at Angie's brain. She tried to understand what she was missing, but it eluded her.

"Do the Crossworts know about the necklace? Could they feel its energy when the box was opened?" Jenna thought they might be on to something. "Is that why they came to town?"

"And what about Walter Withers and Gloria?" Angie offered. "They must be after the necklace, too."

"It has been easy for people to deduce where the necklace might be." Mr. Finch removed his glasses and wiped the lenses with the edge of his sweater. "There have been several newspaper articles about all of us helping to solve recent mysteries in town. Those articles mentioned the Victorian and the B and B. We are pretty easy to find."

Jenna sucked in a breath. "It would also be easy to find out that Tom and I own Katrina Stenmark's former home. All they have to do is look up the land records."

"That's why someone broke into your house." Courtney nodded. "They must have been looking for the necklace."

Jenna's facial muscles tightened in anger. "And that must be why I felt someone watching me while I was working there. They must have been casing the place figuring out when to break in."

"Be sure not to open the box, Miss Ellie," Finch said. "Keeping the box closed will make it much harder, maybe impossible, to find the necklace. Put it somewhere safe." He looked at Jenna. "Perhaps you could see if there's anything on the internet about Katrina Stenmark's death."

"I'm on it." Jenna stood up and went to her laptop.

Courtney looked pensive. "I wonder why someone bothered to threaten us with the burning scarecrows on the common. They threw a firebomb into the house. What's the point? Why not just break in and look for the thing?"

"I bet the sicko wants to scare us first." Courtney gently edged against Euclid trying to get a bit more room in the chair.

"Or maybe they'd like to frighten us into selling and we'll move away." Jenna tapped on her laptop keys. "Maybe the person doesn't want us helping to solve mysteries in town."

Jenna carried her laptop to the sofa and sat down. "There's one small thing on the internet. There's a tiny news story reporting the death of an elderly Sweet Cove woman, Katrina Stenmark. It says Mrs. Stenmark died of natural causes due to an intruder breaking into her home late at night which frightened her into having a heart attack."

Euclid let out a loud hiss making everyone jump.

"I wouldn't call being frightened to death natural causes." Courtney scowled.

"Katrina must have passed the necklace to Nana prior to the person breaking in," Jenna suggested. "I wish we knew more about what happened."

After more discussion, everyone was exhausted and decided to turn in for the night. Angie offered to walk Mr. Finch home and the two stepped out of the Victorian's back door into the dark, chilly air. They headed for the stone walkway that ran from the sisters' house to Mr. Finch's place. The carriage house security light lit up the beginning of the walk and Angie held Finch's arm. The cats followed behind them.

Something caught Angie's eye just as Euclid let out a howling screech that pierced the two people's eardrums. She stopped short and stared up at the oak tree, a gasp escaping from her mouth. She pointed. "Look. The mistletoe."

Mr. Finch's eyes widened like saucers.

All of the mistletoe that was growing in the oak

tree had been cut out. It was gone.

***

THE EARLY morning light filtered into the yard and the four sisters and two cats stood in the back garden staring at the oak tree. A few sprigs of crushed mistletoe lie at the base of the tree. After much speculation and no answers about who and why someone had cut out the mistletoe, Courtney went off to the candy store, Ellie and Angie returned to the house to begin work, and Jenna climbed the staircase and crawled back into bed for three more hours. The cats remained outside for a while scowling up into the oak's branches.

After closing the bake shop at 3pm, Angie met Josh Williams for a bike ride and an early dinner. It was just what she needed to get her mind off the recent events. In the waning light, Josh walked her home from the restaurant. "I'm glad Jack moved Rufus's going away get-together later in the day. I'll head back to the resort to check on things and meet you at Jack's office in thirty minutes." Josh kissed Angie goodbye, and she opened the front door of the Victorian and stepped into the foyer.

The house was oddly quiet. Angie spotted a manila envelope set on the foyer table. A sticky note was attached from Chief Martin saying that the photos from the security camera were inside the envelope and that she and the others should have a look. Angie carried the envelope down the hall to the kitchen and seeing the room empty, she walked to the family room. "Where is everyone?" She called for the cats, but got no response. *They all must have gone to Jack's office already.*

Angie sat down on the sofa, slipped the photos out and spread them on the coffee table. She was surprised to see how snowy and grainy the pictures looked. She squinted trying to make something out. She held one up and moved her face close to the image. Blinking hard several times, she thought she could see a shadowy form. Staring at the photo, she traced her finger along the outlines of a person barely visible. It seemed to be kneeling making an adjustment to something. *Is it wearing a baseball hat?* She looked closer and thought that something hanging down from the neck might be a scarf. Angie sighed disappointed with the poor condition of the photos and how little help they turned out to be.

She got up and went to the foyer and as she was about to climb the steps to her room to change for Rufus's party, she turned her head to the foyer table and saw the baseball cap that Courtney had found in the yard. *The Yankees. New York. It's him.*

Fear and dread put their icy fingers around Angie's throat and nearly choked her.

Her phone buzzed with an incoming text from Ellie. *I'm in the carriage house apartment. I fell. I think I broke my leg.*

Angie took off running.

CHAPTER 24

Angie tore up the stairs to the carriage house apartments. "Ellie!" As soon as the word was out of her mouth, she knew she'd made a mistake. The apartment door flew open and Angie was dragged inside. The slamming of the door made her jump.

Professor Michael Tyler stood before her, his eyes dark with hate. Angie's stomach almost heaved. Her three sisters sat tied up in chairs. She spotted a can of gasoline in the corner that had been in the carriage house garage.

"He used Ellie's phone to text us, too." Courtney glared at the man.

"Quiet," Professor Tyler warned.

Courtney ignored him. "He wants the necklace." She nodded to the door and mouthed the word, 'run.'"

Angie stepped back. Tyler grabbed for her arm, but she swiveled and her fist hit him full in the temple. After a few moments of grappling back and forth, Tyler pulled Angie's arms behind her, pushed her into a chair and bound her to the wooden slats.

Ellie growled, "Don't anyone tell him a thing. Not one thing."

Angie's mind raced. *At least Mr. Finch isn't here. The cats aren't here either.*

Breathing hard, Tyler pulled a knife out of his jacket pocket. His eyes were like sunken holes in his head. He brandished the knife and walked close to Angie, all the while keeping his eyes on Ellie. "Tell me where the necklace is or your pretty sisters won't be pretty anymore."

Ellie's eyes locked onto the knife like lasers. Concentrating with all her energy, her cheeks flushed bright red. The knife started to vibrate in Tyler's hand and he stared with alarm at the thing wobbling and shaking in his grip.

A wild scratching noise could be heard at the window facing the oak tree. Everyone turned towards the sound to see Euclid sitting on a branch just outside the window. He held a white box in his mouth.

Tyler hurried to the window and pushed it open. His eyes glittered crazily at the box between Euclid's teeth. "Nice kitty. Come here."

Euclid glared at the man and then leaped from the branch into the apartment.

"No, Euclid!" Ellie screeched. "Don't let him get the box."

Mr. Finch called from the base of the tree in the dark yard of the garden. "What's going on up there?"

Hearing Finch's voice, Tyler panicked. He grabbed the white box that Euclid had dropped and shoved it into his jeans. Lunging for the gas can, he splashed it around the kitchen area. Sweat poured down the sides of Tyler's face. He pulled a lighter out of his pocket and as he ran for the apartment door, he turned and threw the lighter into the kitchen releasing a fireball into the air.

The force of the ignited gasoline toppled Courtney and Jenna's chairs and the girls, still tied to their seats, slammed onto the living room floor on their sides.

The roar of the flames nearly deafened her, but Angie thought she could hear a siren far off in the distance. Smoke filled the room as the flames roared up the kitchen walls.

A small black figure jumped from the tree branch into the chaos carrying something in her mouth.

"Circe!" Angie's heart nearly burst. Because of the swirling smoke, she couldn't make out what the cat had dropped onto the floor for Euclid, but she could see that they each carried something between their teeth as they raced in circles around and around the sisters still strapped in the chairs.

Angie coughed and her vision dimmed. She knew she was only hallucinating that the smoke and flames were starting to dissipate around them. Her chin fell to her chest and just before she closed her eyes, she felt her heart fill with love for the two crazy cats, her sisters, Mr. Finch, and Josh.

A cracking smash jolted Angie and shook her back to consciousness. Firefighters rushed into the room. The girls were lifted, dragged, and pulled from the space, the flames licking at the walls and ceiling, and they were carried down the staircase and placed onto the lawn on the far side of the yard.

Tears streamed down Mr. Finch's cheeks as he limped from sister to sister, and when he saw that they were alive, he sank down onto the grass and wept, with two slightly singed felines standing with their front paws leaning against him, carefully licking the tears from his wrinkled face.

***

AMBULANCES WERE parked on the street and as the girls sat on the front porch getting checked over by medical personnel, Jack Ford, Rufus, Tom, and Josh lurched to a stop in Tom's truck at the curb in front of the Victorian. With worried looks, they jumped from the vehicle and ran to their girlfriends.

"We didn't know what was going on." Tom held Jenna in his arms.

"When none of you showed up at the going-away gathering for Rufus, we knew something bad had happened." Jack ran his hand over Ellie's hair and she rested her cheek on his chest.

"We texted all of you, but there was no answer."

Josh looked pale sitting next to Angie holding her hand.

"All's well that ends well." Courtney put her hand gently against Rufus' face as he knelt in front of her chair. Thinking of Rufus's next day departure back to England, she added, "Sort of."

Walking away from one of the ambulances, Betty had her arm around Mr. Finch. "I insisted that Victor be checked over. All this excitement for a man of his age...." She clucked and shook her head. "However, he has been pronounced to be fit as a fiddle."

"Physically, anyway." Finch had dark circles under his eyes.

Betty sat the exhausted man in one of the porch rockers. "I'm going to make Victor a hot toddy. Anyone else want one?"

The four men raised their hands. Betty went inside to concoct the beverages. Sure that their sweethearts were fine, Rufus, Tom, Josh, and Jack headed around to the back yard to see the damage to the carriage house.

"We'll be right back." Josh smiled at Angie.

"How did you know we were in the apartment, Mr. Finch?" Ellie asked.

"The cats alerted me. They ran to my back door howling and carrying on. I knew trouble had set foot at the Victorian." Circe climbed onto Finch's lap. Euclid sat on the porch railing, listening.

Finch continued. "I texted all of you, but of

course, there was no reply. I followed the cats to the back of the Victorian and I could see Miss Angie and Professor Tyler upstairs near the carriage house second floor window. I knew the trouble was because of Ellie's necklace. The cats and I went into the house where I called the police. I found the necklace there and took it out of the box. I handed the empty box to Euclid and instructed him to climb the tree up to the window."

Betty came onto the porch carrying a tray with the hot toddies. "How interesting. I didn't know cats would do as someone asked. I thought they only did what they wanted."

Euclid glared at Betty and Angie gave him a warning look.

Betty set the tray down. "Oh, I forgot the cinnamon sticks." She went back into the house.

Mr. Finch said, "I'd found a spring of the mistletoe on the ground. I gave it to Circe and asked her to go up the tree and into the apartment to try to keep the fire away from all of you. She took the plant and grabbed the necklace and up she went to help save you. The cats jumped into the apartment when Tyler opened the window. I could smell smoke, so I called the fire department."

Just as the men came around the corner to the porch, Courtney said, "The cats had mistletoe and Ellie's necklace in their mouths and they ran around us trying to protect us from the fire."

Rufus chuckled. "Maybe they knew that

mistletoe is supposed to ward off fires."

Circe gave the young man a serene look.

Rufus whispered something to Tom. Tom nodded and stood up. "I'll be right back." He winked at Jenna and went to his truck, got in, and drove away."

The girls and Mr. Finch started to feel better as the pleasant company and chatter helped to ease the tension of their ordeal. Having survived the near-fatal attack filled them with equal parts giddiness and crushing fatigue.

Fifteen minutes later, Tom pulled up to the curb and carried something to the porch. It was a banner and Rufus and Jack unrolled it.

"This was hanging up at Jack's office. We wanted to surprise you when you came to the get-together." Rufus smiled at Courtney.

On the banner, the words, "Rufus is Staying" were written in colorful block letters.

Courtney blinked. She looked at the young Englishman. "What?"

"I'm staying." He grinned from ear to ear. "I'll fly back to school a few times to meet with my professors and take the final exam, but otherwise I have permission to complete my final term here through independent study and Skype sessions."

Courtney couldn't believe what Rufus was saying. Her heart did a flip and she hurried to her boyfriend and wrapped him in her arms.

Jack cleared his throat. "In a moment of

weakness, I offered Rufus a job in my firm as an associate."

"And," Rufus smiled. "In a moment of weakness, I accepted."

Courtney whooped and everyone stood. The guys shook hands with Rufus and the women hugged him welcoming the young man to Sweet Cove as a new permanent resident.

Courtney was the second person in the last sixty minutes who had tears of happiness running down her cheeks.

CHAPTER 25

After finishing the hot toddies, the men decided to leave so that the girls and Mr. Finch could rest and recover from the evening's misadventure. The group planned to get-together the next day for a "Count our Blessings" barbecue.

Betty insisted on taking Mr. Finch home. She was going to cook him a warm meal and put him to bed. She kissed his head and took his hand, but before heading to the walkway that led to his house, the four sisters wrapped him in a bear hug and planted kisses on his cheeks.

"I don't know what we'd do without you, Mr. Finch," Ellie said. She winked at the cats. "I'm not sure what we'd do without you two, either."

Finch smiled down at the beautiful cats. "We make a fine team."

Circe followed behind Betty and Finch as they walked slowly home under the stars.

Before heading into the Victorian, the girls stood off to the side watching the firefighters moving about the smoking ruin of their carriage house.

Angie nudged Jenna. "I guess you and Tom won't be moving into the carriage house apartment now, huh."

Jenna couldn't help but chuckle at her sister's lame joke.

"A joke? At a time like this?" Ellie scolded.

"It's *joy* at a time like this." Courtney rubbed her wrist where it had been tied to the chair. "Joy that we're all okay."

Angie smiled. "Mr. Finch would tell us that the carriage house is just wood and paint and that no one can ever take away what's most important to us. With family and friends, we have everything we need."

Police Chief Martin walked up to the girls. He held out the white leather box and handed it to Ellie. "Professor Tyler has been arrested and taken into custody. He burned the scarecrows on the common and he admitted to removing the mistletoe from the tree and throwing the firebomb into your house. He isn't exactly forthcoming about *why* he did the things he did." The chief raised an eyebrow. "Which is probably for the best." One of the firefighters waved the chief over and he excused himself. As he walked away, he sighed. "At least you're all okay."

Angie scowled. "Professor Tyler cut the mistletoe out of the tree so we couldn't use it to help us. He had this all planned. He found the gasoline can in the garage. He asked Ellie if he could rent one of the apartments so he could herd us all up there away from everyone. He was going to kill us so we couldn't implicate him in stealing the necklace and threatening us."

Ellie nodded. "Well, he's caught now. It's finally over."

A voice from the darkness spoke. "It might not be over completely."

The girls turned around to see Gloria standing behind them wearing the long dark coat. They all went to the pergola and took seats in the Adirondack chairs.

"I'm sorry you thought I was behind the trouble, but I had to be careful." Gloria held her hands in her lap.

Courtney asked softly, "You have powers, too?"

Gloria nodded. "Some."

A huge smile spread over Courtney's mouth. "Cool."

"I can only stay for a few minutes. I want to tell you a few things." Gloria leaned forward. "For a time, the necklace was in Katrina Stenmark's possession. She knew that it had powers and that people were after it, so she gave it to your grandmother for safekeeping. Someone broke into Katrina's house trying to find the necklace. Katrina wouldn't tell where it was. She died during the break-in, we aren't sure how, but she protected the necklace with her life."

"Why is the necklace so important?" Ellie asked.

"It has great power. Among other substances, it has mistletoe inside it. The necklace can help with all sorts of things. It can sometimes heal illness, it can protect against fire. I don't know all of its secrets. There are people, like Professor Tyler, who want to possess it and will do anything to get their hands on it." Gloria made eye contact with each sister. "You must keep it out of their hands."

"What about the Crossworts?" Angie asked.

"Mrs. Crosswort was quite ill." Gloria looked at Ellie. "As you've probably figured out, when the necklace is out of the box, its energy can be felt by some. The Crossworts could feel it and came looking for help. I assume Mrs. Crosswort touched the stone?"

Ellie nodded.

"You must have had it on when she touched it?"

Ellie nodded again. Her oval face looked pale in the darkness.

"The necklace is its most powerful in the hands of a keeper, the protector of the stone. It glows and shimmers only when it is held by a keeper." Gloria smiled at Ellie. "The stone knows who it should be with and right now, that's you. By the way, Mrs. Crosswort has been healed. They've already left Sweet Cove."

"Who set the fire at the house next to the Crossworts?" Jenna asked.

Gloria sighed. "Professor Tyler. He thought the Crossworts were living there. He wanted to scare them away from town ... or worse. To keep them from getting at the necklace."

Angie made a face. "Professor Tyler has powers, too?"

Gloria nodded. "He must. When the necklace was removed from the box, he must have felt its energy and then came looking for it."

"He must have used his powers to cause the security cameras to go all snowy while he was on the common setting up the scarecrows and the fire," Angie noted. "At the common, Mr. Finch and I smelled gasoline. I guess that was a premonition of what was to come."

"What about Walter Withers?" Courtney frowned. "Our secret agent."

"Walter is a helper, like me. He came to Sweet Cove specifically to help keep you safe. He moves from place to place, wherever he's needed. He and I were outside the Victorian the night Tyler threw the firebomb into the house. We kept it from igniting." Gloria nodded to the oak tree. "The mistletoe came to help, too. We left sprigs of it out in different places for you to find in order to hint at its usefulness." Gloria stood up. "Keep the necklace out of sight."

"Stay for a while longer," Courtney said. "We have a million questions."

Gloria gave a little shrug and smiled. "Some things you have to discover on your own." She headed for the front of the house. "See you at the salon."

The sisters talked for a while about all that had happened and then decided to go inside, make popcorn, and watch a movie.

"This weekend is the Halloween festival." Jenna put her arm though Angie's. "We can enjoy it without looking over our shoulders all the time."

"I wonder if it's too late to enter a scarecrow in the town contest," Angie said.

The girls glanced at the carriage house as they went into the house through the back door.

"What a mess." Ellie's voice was sad.

"Well," Jenna said, "we can contract with Tom's company to rebuild it."

Angie kidded, "Tom *does* need a new project to keep him busy."

Inside, the girls took showers, put on pajamas, and Jenna, Angie, and Ellie met in the family room.

For a moment, Angie's forehead creased with worry. "Where's the necklace?"

"Don't worry." Ellie plopped on the sofa. "It's in the safe and that's where it's going to stay."

Jenna joined her sister on the couch. "Where's Courtney?"

"Rufus came back," Angie said. "They're out in the garden." She smiled. "I wouldn't wait for her."

✳✳✳

RUFUS AND Courtney had their arms around

each other and she rested her head on his chest as she gazed up at the sky.

"Look at the stars. They're so beautiful tonight."

"I don't need to look at the stars. There's something more beautiful right here in front of me." Rufus held the lovely young woman in his arms and kissed her sweetly standing beneath the branches of the old oak tree right under the spot where the mistletoe used to be.

So absorbed by a certain kind of magic sparking between them, Courtney and Rufus didn't notice that a few feet away in the clear, dark night, two fine felines sat side by side on the stones of the fire pit, watching over the Victorian, and the humans they loved.

THANK YOU FOR READING!

BOOKS BY J.A. WHITING CAN BE FOUND HERE:

www.amazon.com/author/jawhiting

To hear about new books and book sales, please sign up for my mailing list at:

www.jawhitingbooks.com

Your email will never be sold, shared, or spammed.

SWEET COVE COZY MYSTERIES

The Sweet Dreams Bake Shop (Sweet Cove Cozy Mystery Book 1)

Murder So Sweet (Sweet Cove Cozy Mystery Book 2)

Sweet Secrets (Sweet Cove Cozy Mystery Book 3)

Sweet Deceit (Sweet Cove Cozy Mystery Book 4)

Sweetness and Light (Sweet Cove Cozy Mystery

Book 5)

Home Sweet Home (Sweet Cove Cozy Mystery Book 6)

Sweet Fire and Stone (Sweet Cove Cozy Mystery Book 7)

And more to come!

LIN COFFIN COZY MYSTERIES

A Haunted Murder (A Lin Coffin Cozy Mystery Book 1)

A Haunted Disappearance (A Lin Coffin Cozy Mystery Book 2)

The Haunted Bones (A Lin Coffin Cozy Mystery Book 3) early March '16

And more to come!

MYSTERIES

The Killings (Olivia Miller Mystery – Book 1)

Red Julie (Olivia Miller Mystery - Book 2)

The Stone of Sadness (Olivia Miller Mystery - Book 3)

If you enjoyed the book, please consider leaving a review.

A few words are all that's needed.

It would be very much appreciated.

ABOUT THE AUTHOR

J.A. Whiting lives with her family in New England where she works full time in education. Whiting loves reading and writing mystery and suspense stories.

VISIT ME AT:

www.jawhitingbooks.com

www.facebook.com/jawhitingauthor

www.amazon.com/author/jawhiting

SOME RECIPES FROM THE SWEET COVE SERIES

AZTEC PUMPKIN BREAD WITH CHOCOLATE CHIPS

Ingredients

*4 cups all-purpose flour
*2 teaspoons baking soda
*1 teaspoon salt
*1 teaspoon ground cinnamon
*½ - 1 teaspoon ground nutmeg
*½ - 1 teaspoon chipotle chili powder
*2 cups sugar
*¾ cup butter or margarine, softened
*4 eggs
*½ cup water
*1 can (15 oz) pumpkin (don't use pumpkin pie mix)
*1 cup plus 3 tablespoons miniature semisweet or dark chocolate chips
*2 tablespoons chopped nuts (your preference – pecans, walnuts, almonds, etc)

*1 teaspoon sugar

Directions

*Heat oven to 350°F.

*Grease bottom of two 8x4-inch loaf pans with butter and lightly flour (or spray bottoms of the pans with cooking spray and do not flour).

*In medium bowl, stir flour, baking soda, salt, cinnamon, nutmeg, and chili powder until mixed; set aside.

*In large bowl, using an electric mixer on medium, beat 2 cups sugar with the butter for 1-2 minutes or until creamy.

*Add the eggs, one at a time, and beating well after each addition.

*Beat in the water and pumpkin on low speed.

*Add flour mixture; beat on low speed for about 1 minute or until the mixture is moistened.

*Stir in 1 cup of the chocolate chips.

*Spread the mixture evenly between the 2 pans.

*Sprinkle the tops with remaining 3 tablespoons chocolate chips, the nuts and 1 teaspoon sugar.

*Bake 65 minutes to 75 minutes or until toothpick inserted in the center comes out clean.

*Cool the bread in pans for 10-15 minutes

*Remove from pans to cooling rack. Cool completely.

VEGGIE PIE WITH LENTILS AND MASHED POTATOES

Ingredients

*1 Tablespoon olive oil
*1 large onion, sliced
*4 large carrots cut into slices the size of sugar cubes
*6 ounces of red wine
*4 ounces of water
*15-ounce can of chopped tomatoes
*1-2 vegetable stock cubes
*15 ounce can of lentils

Ingredients - Mashed Potato Topping:

*Either use 4 sweet potatoes; or 4 russet potatoes; or 2 potatoes of each kind – peeled and cut into chunks
*2 ounces of butter
*Salt and pepper to taste
*3-6 ounces of shredded Cheddar

Directions

*Heat the oil in a large frying pan

*Fry the onion until it turns golden

*Add the carrots to the frying pan

*Pour in the wine, water, and the tomatoes

*Crumble in the stock cubes and simmer for 10 minutes

*Add the can of lentils, including the juice; cover and simmer for 15 minutes until the carrots are tender

*Boil the potatoes for 15 minutes or until tender and drain well

*Mash with the butter and season with salt and pepper to taste

*Pile the lentil mixture into a pie dish

*Spoon the mashed potatoes over the top

*Sprinkle the cheese over the potatoes

*The pie can be covered and refrigerated for 2 days (can also be frozen for up to a month)

*Heat oven to 375 F

*Cook for 20-30 minutes if cooking right away (or for 45 minutes if it was in the refrigerator) until hot all the way through

APPLE PIE FUDGE

Ingredients

*3 cups White Chocolate Chips
*¾ cups Canned Apple Pie Filling
*3 cups granulated sugar
*¾ cups unsalted butter
*1 pinch salt
*1 cup heavy cream
*1 teaspoon cinnamon
*½ teaspoons ground nutmeg
*½ teaspoons allspice

Directions

*Line an 8×8 baking dish with parchment paper (let the paper hang over two opposite sides of the pan - you will use it as handles to remove the fudge from the pan)

*Add the white chocolate chips and the apple pie filling into a mixing bowl

*In a large saucepan, heat sugar, butter, salt, cream, cinnamon,

nutmeg and allspice over medium heat

*Bring to a rolling boil; Stir continuously for about 4 minutes

*Remove from the heat

*Quickly pour the hot mixture into the prepped mixing bowl with the white chocolate and apple pie filling

*Beat on medium speed until white chocolate is smooth (about 2 minutes)

*Pour it into the prepared baking dish

*Refrigerate for 3 hours, until hardened, or overnight

*Remove fudge from the pan using the parchment paper handles and place it on a cutting board

*Cut fudge into bite sized pieces

*You can also top each square of fudge with a small piece of cookie

pushed into the top (gingersnaps, sugar cookies) broken into bite sized pieces

*Store in a covered container in the refrigerator

*Enjoy within one week or freeze.

VEGAN EASY SPICY (OR NOT) MACARONI AND CHEESE

Ingredients

*8 ounces of your favorite pasta
*1/4 cup unsweetened almond milk or substitute your favorite unsweetened non-dairy milk (If you prefer dairy – use whole or 2 percent milk)
*2 tablespoons olive oil
*2 heaping tablespoons all-purpose flour
*1/2 cup nutritional yeast flakes
*1/2 teaspoon garlic powder
*1/4 teaspoon chili powder (optional if you prefer not spicy)
*1/4 teaspoon chipotle powder (optional)
*Salt, to taste

Directions

*Cook the pasta according to package

*Drain and place back in pot

*In a medium sauce pan, heat oil over medium heat, add flour and whisk

*Continue whisking and cook for 2 minutes.

*Slowly add the milk, whisking constantly

*Turn heat to low and cook until sauce thickens, about 8 minutes, stirring frequently

*Remove from heat

*Stir in nutritional yeast, salt, garlic powder, chili powder (if desired) and chipotle powder (if desired)

*Stir until everything is well-mixed and smooth

*Add sauce to the pasta, toss well, add more milk as needed and serve right away.

NOTE: You may add steamed broccoli, cooked corn or peas,

fried mushrooms, or fried onions and toss well

CARAMEL OAT AND CHOCOLATE CHIP COOKIES

Ingredients

*1 cup all-purpose flour
*¾ cup whole wheat flour
*1 ¾ cup quick oats
*1 tsp baking soda
*½ tsp salt
*¾ cup butter, softened
*½ cup honey
*⅓ cup brown sugar
*2 eggs
*1 tsp vanilla extract
*¾ cup of dark chocolate chips
*½ cup soft caramels, chopped into small pieces

Directions

*Preheat oven to 350 F

*Line a cookie sheet with parchment paper

*In a large bowl, whisk together oats, wheat flour, flour, baking soda, and salt

*In another bowl, use a mixer to cream together the butter, honey, and brown sugar

*Add the eggs and vanilla and beat until the mixture is creamy

*Stir in dry ingredients until well combined

*Stir in the chocolate chips and the pieces of caramels

*Drop the dough with heaping tablespoons onto the cookie sheet

*Bake for 8-10 minutes or until the edges of the cookies start to turn a golden brown

*Remove to a wire rack; Cool for 5-10 minutes

*Store in an airtight container

Made in the USA
Coppell, TX
17 November 2021